RAVEN MOUNTAIN

Sequel to *Green River Saga*
A Mythic Tale

RAVEN MOUNTAIN

Sequel to *Green River Saga*
A Mythic Tale

Michael W. Shurgot

Sunstone Press
Santa Fe

Sunstone books may be purchased for educational, business, or sales promotional use.
For information please write: Special Markets Department, Sunstone Press,
P.O. Box 2321, Santa Fe, New Mexico 87504-2321.

Printed on acid-free paper

eBook 978-1-61139-586-0

Library of Congress Cataloging-in-Publication Data

Names: Shurgot, Michael W., 1943- author.
Title: Raven Mountain : sequel to Green River saga : a mythic tale / Michael W. Shurgot.
Description: Santa Fe : Sunstone Press, [2023] | Summary: "Johnny Redfeather, a Civil War veteran of Irish/Cheyenne heritage, struggles to protect his Indian heritage and adopted family against insurmountable odds"-- Provided by publisher.
Identifiers: LCCN 2023022031 | ISBN 9781632932921 (paperback) | ISBN 9781611395860 (epub)
Subjects: LCSH: Indians--Mixed descent--Fiction. | United States--History--Civil War, 1861-1865--Veterans--Fiction. | LCGFT: Western fiction.
Classification: LCC PS3619.H8676 R38 2023 | DDC 813.6--dc23/eng/20230531

LC record available at https://lccn.loc.gov/2023022031

WWW.SUNSTONEPRESS.COM
SUNSTONE PRESS / POST OFFICE BOX 2321 / SANTA FE, NM 87504-2321 /USA
(505) 988-4418

To:

Nick and Anne
and
Mara and Matt

Blessings Always.

Acknowledgements

The principal sources for information in this novel about Native American and specifically Cheyenne history, language, legends, and mythologies are the following:

Peter Cozzens, *The Earth is Weeping*. New York: Alfred A. Knopf, 2016

Richard Erdoes and Alfonso Ortiz, eds. *American Indian Myths and Legends*. New York: Pantheon Books, 1984

Richard Erdoes, *Crying for a Dream*. Santa Fe: Bear & Company, 1990

Alice Marriott and Carol K. Rachlin, eds. *Plains Indian Mythology*. New York: Thomas Y. Crowell, 1975

Gerry Robinson, *The Cheyenne Story: An Interpretation of Courage*. Helena, MT: Sweetgrass Books, 2019

Grace Jackson Penney, *Tales of the Cheyenne*. Boston: Houghton Mifflin, 1953

www.Native-Languages.org

The Earth is a living thing. The Mountains speak.
The trees sing. Lakes can think. Pebbles have a
soul. Rocks have power.
Lame Deer, Sioux Medicine Man

Mitakuye Oyasin ("All My Relations")
We will live by this word.
We are related to everything.
We are still here.
We shall live!
Lakota Prayer

Hestovatohkeo'o: (English "Two-Face") A huge, malevolent, man-like monster with a second face on the back of his head; a person who makes contact with this second face will be murdered by the monster, who tries many ploys to try to get his victims to look at him.
Native Languages of the Americas: Cheyenne Legends, Myths, and Stories

The need 'to get even,' to repay in kind, to hurt the enemy, may be so compelling that it assumes the character of a must, an ought force which is right and proper.
Fritz Heider, *The Psychology of Interpersonal Relations*

Revenge is essentially rooted in the feeling of power and superiority.
Edward Westermarck, *Ethical Relativity*

Prologue
Johnny Redfeather's Journey

In November, 1864 Johnny O'Shaughnessy Redfeather and Colonel William Swanson, with several of his men, escaped Camp Lawton Prison in Georgia. Just before returning to Swanson's garrison, Redfeather abandoned him, telling him that he could remain with neither Union nor Confederate soldiers. "They all want my scalp now," Redfeather had insisted. "I'll be all go to hell. I got to strike out on my own in these mountains, try to get to Indian country out west quickly as possible. You guard your Union ass, Swanson," Redfeather told him, "and don't worry about me. I know how to survive in these mountains all right. Indians good at that. And you got no god-damn idea where I am, right?"

"Right, Johnny. Sure am obliged. My men and I thank you for freeing us the way you did. I don't guess I'll ever see you again, but if any man can survive out here on his own, I suspect it's you all right. And yeah, I got no god-damn idea where you're off to. Just keep your head down, Johnny Redfeather."

"I sure will. You do the same. Now I got to go!" Swanson extended his hand, and Redfeather grabbed him firmly by his forearm. Though initially surprised, Swanson realized Redfeather's intent, and grabbed his forearm. They held their grip for a few seconds, then Redfeather let go, saluted Swanson, and disappeared into the surrounding forest.

For nearly two years Redfeather lived by his wits and daring as he journeyed north and west through parts of Kansas, Colorado, and Dakota Territories, seeking to find the tribe of his mother, the daughter of a Medicine Man: The Cheyenne People. Along the way he lived and often hunted with members of several tribes in the Kansas and Colorado Territories, including Cherokee, Shawnee, Osage, Kiowa, and Arapaho Indians. He arrived in Green River, Wyoming in early March, 1866 and spent time with Running Bear's tribe of Southern Cheyenne in Reiser Canyon, northeast of Green River.

Being of mixed heritage—Indian and Irish—he also ingratiated himself with several white people in the community, especially Sheriff Jim Talbot, the only white lawman Redfeather had ever respected. He began spending time in the town's two saloons, Hal's and especially Milly's Green River Saloon. In September, 1866 he helped defend Milly's against an attack by a gang of drunken herders and railroad workers incited by the cattle rancher Brent Tompkin. He saved the Sheriff's life during that attack, and again in early April, 1867 during Tompkin's murderous siege at Running Bear's Cheyenne encampment in Reiser Canyon

Now, with Running Bear's tribe vanquished, and its few remaining members scattered he knew not where among the mountains north and west of Green River, Johnny Redfeather felt alone and scared. He hunted and trapped in the mountains, and sold carcasses to establishments in town to buy the liquor and laudanum with which he medicated his loneliness. In his cabin tucked behind Raven Mountain where, he believed, no white man would ever venture, he felt secure only in that part of himself that he could still identify as Indian, even as he sensed that identity slowly eroding beyond his control.

1
Lamentations; April 18, 1867

All our enemies have opened their mouths against us. Fear and a snare is come upon us, desolation and destruction.
The Lamentations of Jeremiah 3: 46-47

Just above the rim of Eagle Canyon Johnny Redfeather stood for several minutes against the increasing intensity of an early spring thunder storm. Wind gusts lacerated the budding trees near the canyon rim, and blew rain into his face. Still he did not move. Mist billowed from the enormous canyon below him, gradually enveloping him in its folds, obscuring the contours of the rock formations on either side of him. Redfeather remained immobile, as if wishing to be swallowed by the swirling mist. His horse, puzzled by such a long silence, whinnied behind him, perhaps wondering aloud when they would ride again.

On the cliff to his right and above, a Southern Cheyenne woman wrapped her son in a heavy wool blanket and held him tightly against her body. Rain gathered in droplets on her cheek bones, then rolled down her face onto the head of her shivering child. She bowed her head into her son's blanket, and wept. Her shoulders began shaking and, as she gasped for breath, grief ravaged her entire body and she fell to her knees, still clinging desperately to her child. She wailed hideously to the wind and the rain as if the elements could comprehend her loss and mend her pain.

Hearing the woman's ghostly screams Redfeather turned toward the cliff where the woman's huddled form gradually emerged in the rain. He walked slowly up the trail on the far side of the canyon toward the wordless sounds he nonetheless understood all too plainly. As he approached the woman and her child, a lone Indian warrior emerged from around a boulder, pointing his rifle squarely at Redfeather.

"I'm meaning no harm," Redfeather yelled. "Just thought I could help, that's all."

The woman turned toward the two men. "No," she cried frantically. "This is Redfeather. You know him."

Although the warrior recognized Redfeather from his recent visits to Running Bear's eviscerated encampment in Reiser Canyon, he nonetheless still aimed his rifle at Redfeather's head.

"You with the white man, the sheriff, before he left?"

"Sheriff Talbot's not here now," Redfeather explained. "Headed back to town, honest. I just brought him here to see the canyon."

The woman reached out to Redfeather and held his left arm. "You come with us. Yes? To the canyon, to see Running Bear. No harm, no guns." She looked at the warrior, nodded, and motioned downward. The warrior lowered his rifle.

Relieved, Redfeather touched the woman's hand on his sleeve. "Thanks. Good. I'll just go get my horse. You all go on ahead, I'll follow, seeing as I know the way well enough by now."

The warrior nodded. Still eyeing Redfeather, he propped his rifle against a rock. He helped the woman and her son up onto his horse, then grabbed the rifle and swiftly swung up behind them. He looked down at Redfeather, then turned his horse and steered it down toward the rim of the canyon. Redfeather watched them ride slowly away through the increasing rain and swirling winds.

"Poor damn Cheyenne," he muttered. "Epevo'eha, broken to pieces. Haven't got one good chance left. Least ways not out here." He returned to his horse, mounted, and began riding slowly toward Reiser Canyon. "God-damn Ve'ho'e, white men!" he spat as he rode, and wept.

2
Milly's Green River Saloon

Sheriff Jim Talbot had left Eagle Canyon moments before Redfeather encountered the Indian woman and the warrior at the canyon's rim. He rode slowly southeast from Eagle Canyon toward Green River. The storm passed as quickly as it erupted, the early spring sun was already high, and Talbot welcomed its warmth on his body. Around him the vegetation that struggles to survive in the blistering summers and brutal winters of the plains and high mountains was blooming. Rivulets of melting snow from the surrounding peaks careened together below to form impromptu streams that rushed around rocks and surged into long dry arroyos. As he rode he thought about the beauty and mystery of the huge canyon he had just left. He thought too of Johnny Redfeather, wondering where he would ride, what country he would seek, what solace even this ripening spring now surrounding him could possibly offer to him. Talbot feared that he was now hopelessly lost amid this vast, indifferent wilderness. He knew that Redfeather's soul, if not his mind, was scarred beyond any conceivable medicine that he or a doctor or even Running Bear might provide. As if any of them had anything to offer.

In town he stopped near the round-about at a crossroads just half a mile up a dusty street from his office. He dismounted and sat down on the bench encircling a wooden statue of a white man and an Indian clasping each other's forearm. Johnny Redfeather had used that grip on him at Milly's last September after together they vanquished an attack on her saloon led by Brent Tompkin, a vicious cattle rancher. Talbot's memory of that moment was always invigorating, and he again admired the twin figures, locked arm-in-arm, embodying in seemingly impervious oak the ideals of cooperation and brotherhood.

Yet the statue now seemed hideously irrelevant. The slaughter of Running Bear's tribe—men, women, children—in Reiser Canyon two weeks before by a mob of herders and railroad workers led by Tompkin haunted him, and he knew it always would. For the hundredth time he asked himself why he had not done more to prevent that attack. Why he had not requested a larger posse from Fort Laramie earlier in the spring, and why, above all, he had never suspected that Tompkin would actually attack Running Bear's encampment? If he was the white man of the statue, who now was the Indian? Running Bear? Johnny Redfeather? White people's vague idea of a conquered, complacent Indian Chief from some local tribe that no longer "caused trouble" for settlers, especially cattle men, railroad workers, and miners? Men who understood neither reason nor charity and delegated themselves as law-givers? Talbot rose, mounted his horse, and began riding slowly toward Milly's Saloon, where he expected to find his deputy Butch Grogan.

§

Talbot walked through the swinging doors into Milly's Green River Saloon twenty minutes later. What one inebriated customer had once described as a "cathedral of a cathouse," it was located in the center of town on the main, north-south running street. Its two floors towered over every other structure nearby, and was easily the building one first noticed when entering town from either direction. Talbot always marveled at Milly's attempt to "fancy up" the place, as she called it. The swinging doors were always freshly painted, and, despite the dust, Milly kept her windows clean, especially all the new ones she needed to install after Tompkin's attack. "Windows are too damn expensive to have a bunch of drunken idiots shoot them up!" she often exclaimed. Gas lights flickered every evening from the huge oak supporting beams on the first floor, creating a welcoming, lively atmosphere.

Milly tied red and white bunting every few feet on the railings by the stairs that led to the ladies' rooms on the second floor. "Like a real 'pleasure palace,' like in New Orleans," Milly explained to her husband Frank. "Have to keep it festive!" White wallpaper with flowery designs decorated the walls on both the first and second floors. Oak chairs and tables, several adorned with white linen cloths and small candles for evening dining, were positioned strategically around the main floor, allowing room for energetic dancing and also for her waitresses to maneuver around the floor serving orders for food and liquor. In a far corner stood several gaming tables and chairs, and built into the wall above them was a shelf that held the gamblers' whiskey bottles. On busy weekend nights Roxy, one of Milly's bar maids, accompanied by Deputy Grogan, was always assigned to maintain the supply of liquor to this area. Grogan's presence assured the often-inebriated gamblers that Roxy wouldn't start pouring whiskey until someone had paid for it.

The numerous stools aligned in front of the bar were made of stained white pine, but the long bar was solid oak, and Frank insisted that his was the most consistently polished bar in the entire Dakota Territory. Behind the bar were racks holding a dozen whiskey bottles, and beneath the racks Frank always kept two kegs of beer. Also a loaded shotgun; just in case. Not to be outdone, Milly was as proud of her "ladies" as Frank was of his bar. On busy weekend nights, the ladies all wore paintbrush flowers in their hair and white cotton dresses, low-cut and sporting bright, floral designs, that billowed at their waist and whirled when they danced with the patrons. Many of them, though not all, accepted cash offers stuffed into their bosoms in exchange for room numbers for later in the evening. It was this "entertainment feature" of Milly's festive "establishment," combined of course with the vast amounts of liquor her patrons consumed, that endlessly infuriated Reverend Bartholomew Aloysius Simpson, pastor of Green River Presbyterian Church located just down the street and over two blocks from Milly's. For several months Reverend Simpson had conducted his own peculiar "raids" on Milly's saloon with the dedicated ladies of his Army of the Righteous. This army tried every Sunday evening at precisely seven o'clock to close down her "den of iniquity" and to march all therein off to his church for baptism and spiritual salvation. The saloon's resistance to Simpson's redemption, led by the hysterical antics of Snuffy, the thirteen-year old orphan whose mother had worked briefly at the saloon and whom Milly and her ladies tried to discipline, always frustrated him. Talbot reflected that Reverend Simpson's continual failures had softened somewhat his ardor. The whole town, he believed, was the better for his recent restraint.

Talbot noticed Marilee as soon as he entered. She was wiping down tables and rearranging chairs around the large central area that Milly had begun calling her "dining room" after the crowd she had so successfully entertained last New Year's Eve. Every time Talbot had visited Milly's since that large holiday party, Milly had reminded him of the marvelous time she and Frank, and of course the piano player Charley and guitar player Old Willie and her girls, had enjoyed that night.

"Damn fine time that night, for sure, even if I do have to say so myself," Milly would remark to Talbot almost as soon as he entered, even before he had time to sit down at the bar or grab a table if Grogan were with him. "Marilee keeps talking about it, says she was glad you were here that night. Says it was the best damn New Year's Eve she can remember, not counting of course all the ones she can't remember. But we all got a bunch of them, haven't we?"

"Yes, suppose we do," Talbot would respond, aware that Milly was again reminding him of what she had seen transpire between him and Marilee that night just before everyone raised their glasses and gathered around the bar to welcome the new year. Talbot had spoken to Marilee a few times since during the winter months, especially when he stayed late on Friday and Saturday nights just to keep the peace, but he had not attempted to revisit their quiet conversation, or her gentle stroke of his cheek, just before the clock struck midnight. Since the sudden death of his wife Abigail in July, 1866, Talbot had not allowed himself to imagine a serious relationship. Not with Marilee, not with any woman.

Recently nights at Milly's had been fairly quiet. Talbot still liked to come by occasionally, mostly to chat with Milly and Frank, and on weekend evenings he still enjoyed listening to whatever resemblances to music Charley was able to excavate from his decrepit piano. Old Willie, wearing the cock-eyed, greasy top hat and threadbare clothes that barely clung to his emaciated frame, sat in his usual corner strumming haphazardly as he tried to follow whatever melody he imagined Charley might be playing. Talbot found the resulting cacophony oddly comforting, an innocent echo of the disorder he had experienced since becoming Sheriff. Charley and Old Willie, he thought, could bang and strum away all they liked.

"Why Sheriff Talbot, I do declare. Nice to see you again. Isn't this a fine spring day?" Marilee greeted Talbot as he stepped between two tables she was cleaning. He ran his finger down the top of one, eyed it, then declared, "Spotless! Well done, Marilee."

"Yeah, real hard to do, isn't it? Wipe down a bunch of tables with a wet cloth and then rinse out all the spilled whiskey. Lord but I am good at this!"

"Aw Marilee, I am sorry. I was just trying to complement you. Be friendly. I meant no harm, none at all."

"Yeah, well, between your 'compliments' for cleaning up slop and grubby men asking me for a room number every night and shoving bills down the front my dress with their filthy hands and swishing around in there for what they think they're fixing to buy, seems a girl can't do anything worthwhile in here. Lord but I get sick of this saloon sometimes. Sick of them fancy ladies up at the hair saloon too, always talking down to me about being one of 'Milly's girls,' like we were just trash. Like the whores that prowl around Hal's no-good saloon, as Milly always calls it. Well, I could tell some stories about those fancy ladies' husbands, let me tell you."

"Well, given who I see in here some Saturday nights, I bet you could."

"Yep, wouldn't be pretty stories, either."

"No, don't suppose they would be. Say, is Milly around?"

"Yeah, back in the kitchen somewhere I think. Frank's out back with Old Willie. Seems he cut his finger real bad chopping wood this morning. Frank figures now he won't be able to play that guitar of his for a while, or maybe not at all. Not that he ever could really. Might be a blessing, Frank figures."

"Well, Frank might have something there all right. Can't say I ever recognized what you could call a 'tune' coming from that beat up old guitar. Must be older than he is. Anyone ever figure where he got that thing, or for that matter, where the hell he came from? He sure seems like a real drifter, like that tumbleweed out there on those plains. Say, any coffee left? I sure could use a big cup."

"Don't know anything about either Willie or his guitar, but I do think there's bound to be some coffee left back behind the bar somewhere. Probably by this time in the day strong enough to kill a man. Best be careful. We don't take responsibility for death by coffee around here. You want a cup I'll go see what I can find, bring it out to this table I'm cleaning, like you say 'really good.'"

Sheriff Talbot sighed, lowered his head, then looked up at Marilee. "Seems I got to learn about how to talk to a woman all over again. I must've forgotten everything Abigail taught me about that since she died. I sure am sorry. As I said, meant no offense."

"That all you forgot? Seems you might recall some other things a woman can teach a man. I'd be surprised if you can't recall just a few. But then, like you said last New Year's Eve, you got work on your mind most of the time, like keeping the peace in this dusty wreck of a town. Guess you haven't forgotten anything about that, now have you?"

"Marilee, Butch and I are the only law around here for God knows how many miles in any direction. Yes, that does occupy a lot of my time, even with Tompkin gone. I don't rightly feel I have to apologize for that fact, and I keep trying and failing to forgive myself for Abigail's death. That still weighs terribly heavy, always will I believe. I know you don't understand that, but maybe you could try to appreciate what I'm saying. Now I believe I'll just go find Milly."

Marilee walked up to Talbot and put her hands on his chest. She pulled the collars of his shirt together at the top, and adjusted the frayed bandana around his neck. "Sheriff, I don't suppose I do understand, at least not fully. Abigail always did call you 'Gentleman Jim,' and last New Year's I guess I finally understood why. I wish you'd stop just one minute and ask yourself exactly why I said to you what I did that night. All of it. It wasn't just for that one night. It was for a whole lot more. Maybe someday you'll understand that. Lord knows you're not stupid, but you turn away from happiness for too long and it just might decide not to come looking for you anymore. Now I'll go see about that mug of coffee."

Talbot watched Marilee walk away from him, then started for the back of the saloon. "Damn pretty woman, I'll have to admit," he thought as he headed around the bar. He found Milly washing out a pile of pots and pans.

"Well, land sakes alive, Sheriff Jim Talbot, isn't it good to see you back here! Grogan been in once or twice, but I wasn't sure you'd ever be back. Grogan said last night that today's the date you were planning on meeting Redfeather up at Eagle Canyon. He hasn't been back here either, though there's a gal here, the one he always calls Darla, who's got some news she says he ought to know about. Sooner the better I'd say. He coming back to town you figure?"

"Don't know, Milly. I think he spends most of his time up in Reiser Canyon at Running Bear's campsite, or what's left of it. I've seen him there a few times when I visited. We don't talk much. I know he blames me for being too late to save Running Bear and his warriors, and I don't blame him for that. He let me know that again today up at Eagle Canyon. Seems sometimes like everything I've done since I got here nearly a year ago has gone wrong in every which way it could. I couldn't save Abigail and I couldn't save Running Bear either. Makes me wonder what this little tin badge is for. Johnny said, by the way, he might come back to get Snuffy, talked about going off somewhere with her. Maybe Old Willie too, though I don't know why."

"Well, maybe Johnny got a few things figured out about that damn rascal. I sure wouldn't mind seeing her go, though she can be entertaining when she wants to be. Especially with that old Reverend Simpson. Damn fool coming around trying to preach to all us 'sinners,' like he called us. Like big old Jupiter used to say, 'Gettin' all up in our business.' Sure did like the way Snuffy stood up to him some nights."

"Yeah, some nights Snuffy really put on a show. Entertained the whole saloon."

"So, you been to Reiser Canyon then? With those Indians? I heard it was really bad. I sure am sorry."

"Yeah, so am I. Always will be. Terrible mess there. Senseless slaughter, just senseless. Seems now like the fighting I did in that war is following me every which way I turn. Anyway, I left Captain Wheeler and about half his posse camped near the canyon entrance, just to make sure none of those brutes returned looking for revenge. I'm sure we didn't kill all of them. I saw some run back up that north side of the canyon trying to escape our cross-fire, but I don't know where they went. Don't care either. They can starve up there in those canyons. Serve them right."

"Yeah, I hear you. Seems like that statue Frank and I put at the crossroads isn't doing much good these days. Don't know where all this is heading now. Speaking of that statue, what about Johnny? How is he?"

"Well, I left him about two hours ago. A storm was coming, but he wanted to stay at the canyon. So I just let him be. I expect he may have gone back to Reiser Canyon. I have to tell you, Milly, during the attack Johnny cut Tompkin's throat just as he was about to shoot me. I now owe him my life twice. I swear that man is magical. Don't rightly know how I'm supposed to pay him back."

"Well, you wait long enough, a time might just come. Seems you best be there when that time comes, because it will come. And you can fry bacon on that one. Speaking of which, we got some left from this morning. Want some? And here comes Marilee with what I guess is some of Frank's coffee from earlier. I'd be really careful with that if I were you. Drink too much it might kill you, though don't tell Frank I said that. But it sure beats nothing."

"Sheriff, here's that coffee I promised you," said Marilee as she handed Talbot a large mug of steaming liquid. "Thought you were coming back to that table I was cleaning. You still want it?"

"Sure Marilee. Thanks. Just gabbing too long here with Milly, mostly about Johnny Redfeather, and seeing how everyone is getting on. Haven't been in town much lately, as you know, mostly holed up in our—er—my cabin at Brown's Wash, riding up to Reiser Canyon a few times. A field of death like I haven't seen since the war. You know, Milly, maybe that's why I still wear this badge. Keep telling myself it's a bet against more killing even though I know damn well it isn't."

"Well, Sheriff," Milly sighed, "you keep telling yourself that so there's a reason for you to remain here. Frank and I and Marilee, all of us, are always glad you're here, as I guess I've told you a hundred times by now."

"Yes, guess you have, and I do appreciate that, believe me. Now let's see about some of that bacon you're always swearing on. Marilee, thanks again for this coffee, even if it might be nearly fatal. Hope to see you around more often now."

"That'd be right nice of you, Sheriff. I sure will look forward to that," Marilee said. Talbot watched her walk away toward the cluster of tables she had been cleaning earlier. "Very pretty indeed," he mused again.

3
Hal's Saloon

Since the top hinges had rusted away, the cracked, bullet-riddled door of Hal's Saloon hung by just the lowest hinge to its rotting frame. Jake Bulger, a large, burly man with a severely pock-marked face and long scraggly beard, wearing a tattered shirt, ragged pants, and worn leather boots leaned hard into the door. As he did it tilted downward and scraped exposed nails on the deeply-worn floor boards. The door suddenly jammed, knocking Bulger backward before he angrily shoved the door so hard that it wobbled on its remaining hinge before slamming into a table behind it.

"Hal," Bulger roared as he stumbled to the bar, "when you gonna fix that god-damn door? Gonna kill somebody someday!"

"You pay me double for your whiskey and I'll fix that damn door. Costs money you know."

"Shit, hinge don't cost nothin'. You're just too god-damn cheap, that's all," Bulger exclaimed as he approached the bar. "Gimme a whiskey, and don't charge me double for it. I'm not payin' for your repairs in this dump."

"Well I'll be damned, if it isn't Jake Bulger!" a voice yelled as Bulger downed his whiskey. A tall, thin man named Jeb Carlson, wearing a dark blue denim shirt, black leather pants, pointed-toe boots, a wide-brimmed hat, and carrying a pistol jammed into a holster on his left hip ambled toward Bulger at the bar. "So, where the hell you been? Just about everyone I know assumed you were killed up at Reiser Canyon in that awful gun battle we all heard about. How'd you escape? You run away?"

"I don't run from nothin,' Carlson! God-damn posse arrived just as we were heading down on them Indians. We all charged down from the north ridge, and just as we got to the Indians' camp in the valley that damn Sheriff and his posse caught us in a cross-fire, and we had no way to escape. Most everybody dead, near as I can tell, including Tompkin. Some guy wearing a grey Confederate coat cut his throat wide open and just left him there, bleeding to death. That lousy coward Curly run off as soon as Talbot's men started firing, and I got no idea what happened to him. Dead somewhere I suppose. I see no way he would still be alive. He never came back to Tompkin's bunkhouse, and the Indians would scalp him sure as shit."

"You're god-damn right there. I told O'Sullivan that Tompkin's plan wouldn't work. Crazy man going after Indians like he was some sort of law all by himself. Damn fool! I told O'Sullivan there's no way I'm riding into an Indian camp trying to fight a bunch of warriors. Dumb as hell I told him. Heard O'Sullivan was killed too. One of the track crew went up there, found his body. Said he's never seen so many bullet holes in one man's body before. So, what's your story?"

"I got back up that ridge once I saw it was hopeless. One of O'Sullivan's men started a fire, and it burned out of control real fast, burning teepees, woman and kids running around screaming. Pure chaos! Never seen anything like it! After all the shooting stopped Running Bear came out of his log house carrying a kid in his arms, wailing like a mad man. He and some warriors and that guy in the Confederate coat went back up the stream with the body. Didn't see them come back. Some medical man and two women arrived in a buggy and tried to save some of the wounded Indians. Later Talbot rode back into the camp with an Indian woman and a boy on his horse, and a dead body on another horse he was leading. I couldn't see for sure, but I figured that might be that god-damn traitor Staggart. I thought I saw him ride away with the woman and kid on his horse just before I headed back up the ridge. I stayed up there for a night, then rode back to Tompkin's bunkhouse. Only a few herders left there, those that weren't on the raid. And I haven't been to town since."

Carlson looked directly at Bulger. "Jake, let me get this straight. You said you saw a guy in a Confederate coat kill Tompkin and then later ride away with some surviving Indians, including the chief? That right? "

"Yeah, that's right. Don't think I've seen one of them grey coats since the war ended. Sure didn't expect to see one in a battle with them Indians. Army men out here mostly from the Union side. Why?"

"Jake, that guy in the Confederate coat was Johnny Redfeather. He's a mixed-breed used to come in here a lot, drinking himself half crazy. Haven't seen him in here too often since that raid on Milly's Saloon. But if this guy you saw kill Tompkin and then go off with the Indians was wearing a Confederate grey, that was Redfeather."

"Redfeather! Redfeather! You sure that's who it was? Johnny Redfeather?"

"Yeah, I'm sure. Haven't you heard about him? Hal says he lives somewhere around here, maybe up in the canyons. Nobody is quite sure where. He seems to just come out of nowhere whenever it suits him. None of Tompkin's men ever mention him? Seems you would have heard of him by now."

"Nah. Like I told you, I only just started workin' for Tompkin in late February. Nobody in the bunkhouse mentioned anything about him since then."

Carlson leaned on his elbow, signaled to Hal for two more whiskies, then glared at Bulger. "So, seems this Red Indian fella is quite important to you? Mind if I ask why?"

"Back in sixty-four, early November, just before that bastard Sherman got to Savannah, late one night Johnny Redfeather and a Union colonel named Swanson escaped together with others from the prison at Camp Lawton, down in Georgia, where my brother Hank and I worked. Several dead guards were found in their cell, and one of the wounded who survived said that Redfeather grabbed a guard's guns and started firing, killed several in seconds. He also said Redfeather killed Hank, who was on duty that night, but not with a gun. He slit Hank's throat and just left him to bleed to death, just like I saw Redfeather slash Tompkin's neck up at Reiser Canyon. Shit! Never did figure out exactly how they escaped, but neither of them was ever seen again. Certainly nowhere in Georgia that I ever heard of."

"Well, that story sounds like Redfeather, all right. Sheriff Talbot told me once that when Tompkin's gang attacked Milly's Saloon, Redfeather came crashing through a window and started firing with two guns he kept low on his hips. Sheriff said Redfeather would 'cross-draw' both guns at once, left side gun with right hand, right side gun with left hand, and was down-right scary accurate with both pistols. Fast as lightning, Talbot said. So shooting a bunch of guards doesn't surprise me at all. Man was a killing machine."

"So he's here, in Green River? How do you know him, might I ask?

You never mentioned him when I was in here before."

"I and a few other guys sometimes ride out with the track workers, providing protection from Indians, grizzly bears, mountain lions, snakes, whatever else tries to get in their way. Redfeather occasionally goes with us if he's around and we think we'll have to talk with Indians instead of just shooting at them. None of them want what they call the 'fire wagon' in their hunting grounds. But the trains got to get through. They're coming this way fast, whether the Indians want them or not."

"I see. What about this Swanson guy? He ever show up around these parts? Maybe with Redfeather?"

"Never met him, so wouldn't recognize him anywhere. Redfeather never said anything about him whenever he's been in here. You curious about him too?"

"Might be. Seein' as how he escaped with Redfeather, and probably killed some of them guards at Lawton. But Redfeather is mainly the one I'm after. Not right, even in war, what he did to Hank. Just let him bleed to death like that. That prison wasn't a real bad place, though I heard some of the guards were pretty vicious to Yanks. Revenge I guess, seeing as how Sherman was comin' on them really fast. But still—my little brother! To die that way...."

"Well, yeah, lots of men died horrible in that war. Same everywhere I guess. I came west from Carolina once it was over, figured there was nothing left for me there. Worked my way here, found good work with the railroad, enough for room and board and whiskey. Don't need much else. So, you still riding with that herd now that Tompkin and I gather most of his men are gone?"

"Yeah, a Kansas guy, Smith, arrived about a week ago, brought some herders with him so's we got enough men now. He's all right, I guess. Yank I gather, but most don't care much about that anymore. Say, Carlson, you ever see Redfeather around these parts, or even in here, would you mind letting me know? I'm mostly out herding now, but still back at the big bunkhouse some nights. I'd sure appreciate knowing where I can find that Indian. Seems he and I got a score to settle."

"Well, Jake, now listen to me. I'm a Rebel like you, but I don't rightly know about even thinking about any kind of revenge now that the war and all that killing is over. I want no part in whatever you might be thinking once you find Redfeather, if you do, but I guess that's between you and him. If I see him in here, or learn of his whereabouts, I'll try to let you know. You might try Milly's Saloon too. That's a whole lot fancier than this joint. At least that's what Milly would tell you. Decent food too, nice tables and chairs to sit at, not like these damn splintered, broken things in here. Doors actually got hinges too, if you can believe that. Real pretty girls too for asking and a few dollars shoved down their fancy dresses. Anyway, like I said, I haven't seen Redfeather anywhere in town since I heard about the attack up in Reiser Canyon. But keep me out of any plans. I want no more killing if I can help it."

"I hear you. Just tell me if you learn where I can find him. I'm not asking for anything more. Promise."

"Deal. How about another whiskey?"

"Fine idea. Thanks."

4
Raven Mountain

Raven Mountain, nearly 7,000 majestic feet high, looms over the expansive foothills and meadow below. Eons ago raging rivers cascading from multiple glaciers near the summit carved deep gouges into the rock, creating a forbidding western wall. On this late April afternoon the massive wall, which drops precipitously two thousand feet to snowfields below, was still shrouded in a wintry haze. Sunlight glistened off high glaciers clinging to rock formations on either side of the vertical spine that divides the wall neatly in half. Gigantic boulders, hurled down the mountain each spring by the constantly shifting glaciers, littered the lower expanses of the snowfields. In the apron of brown foothills sloping toward the meadow, pungent sage caressed the air, and in the lower meadow sprouts of red and orange paintbrush, blue lupine, bitterroot and glacier lilies were punching through the remaining snow-cover to savor the visiting sun. Further down, the extensive forest that stretched to the fast-flowing Green River and the nearby town boasted abundant new growth among its coniferous and deciduous trees.

"Dead Man's Wall," reflected Johnny Redfeather, as he gazed at the treacherous solemnity that dominated this vast wilderness creeping toward spring. He recalled legends of Indians, Cheyenne probably, maybe some others, and also a few white men, who died trying to scale an impossibly steep, treacherous route straight up the rock-face. "An insult to the mountain, going right at it," he reflected. "Find another way, show the mountain some respect. Don't be a fool. Raven Mountain, the Cheyenne say. The bird knows who is welcome, who is not," he thought, as he gazed toward the summit.

Except for his horse, and whatever other creatures might be lurking unseen in the vicinity, Redfeather was alone with the mountain and its domain, just as he liked it. His horse plodded along the narrow trail that began outside town and leads to the forest, then through to the lovely meadow, finally reaching the sandy-colored foothills leading to the base of the mountain. The trail then curls south-east before rising steeply to a mesa on the mountain's southern flank where the path again rises sharply. From the mesa the trail continues north up toward the snow-covered summit, becoming more treacherous with every step even with the sun's warmth. Melting snow churning from above carved fissures across the trail, its spray making the larger rocks especially slippery. After an hour's climb up the steep slope Redfeather dismounted, then led his horse the reminder of the way upward. In the higher elevations snow that had melted earlier in the day was now freezing quickly, covering rocks strewn about the trail with a deadly glaze that at any moment could send him, and possibly also his horse, tumbling toward, if not over, the steep ridge to his left. "Show the mountain respect all right," Redfeather said aloud, as if complaining to the wilderness for having not thought of Indians and their horses when it shaped this rocky monster. "Still, this isn't easy. I'll be all go to hell! Too damn steep and slippery."

He reached the summit four hours after leaving the meadow, drenched in sweat but also acutely aware of the dropping temperature and the sun's gradual decline. From the summit the trail winds nearly two thousand feet down the more gradually sloping east side of the mountain. He knew he had to reach his cabin by nightfall, or risk walking the twisting, icy trail in darkness in freezing air that, even in late spring, envelopes mountains soon after sunset. He walked quickly now, paradoxically content to be alone but simultaneously aware of the many dangers that mountains present, especially as nightfall approaches. A week earlier he had spotted a grizzly sow with two cubs foraging for berries as he descended toward the meadow, and he knew that cougars often roamed the higher elevations hunting elk and deer in spring, often preying on newborn calves. As secure as he felt amid this wilderness, sufficiently distant from the white men—loggers, miners, and herders in Green River determined to overrun every part of Indian country—he did not want to become a sacrificial victim of the mountain's occasional wrath against invaders, even if they were Indians.

As the last golden rays of the sun danced above him along the mountain peak, Redfeather reached his destination, a secluded, ramshackle cabin nestled among a clump of white pines on a plateau above a deep valley below. He tethered his horse to a post near the cabin entrance, both grateful to have arrived at their abode. Sheaves of the thatched roof dangled haphazardly over the cabin's entrance and sides. Wooden planks he had scrounged from another abandoned cabin in the meadow were nailed across the structure's original logs at various angles to stabilize them. A narrow chimney protruded just above the roof line at the back. The front door was three large logs split and wrapped in rope and held together by planks nailed across the top, middle and bottom, and two logs roped together formed the front step. The six-pointed rack of an elk lay against the front wall under a framed opening covered in cowhide.

Redfeather had recently repaired some of the walls with downed logs that he had collected several months ago from a debris pile after a fire had swept partly up the south wall of a nearby canyon. He had hewed and notched the logs with a hatchet his Irish father had given him in Florida when he was a boy. The handle was carved with intricate designs that his father told him were symbols of ancient Irish deities. His father had admonished him never to lose the tool or to let it fall into another's hand, for to do so would anger powerful deities.

Johnny thus believed that the hatchet was magical and when in his possession would save him from harm. He had carried it with him throughout the war and had used it in self-defense, especially during his encounters with bears and mountain lions, and a few white men, during the months near the end of the war when he had wandered alone in the Georgia mountains and beyond before arriving in Indian country. The weapon hung on a hook on the back wall of the cabin, and it was always the first item he saw when he entered. "Hasn't been disturbed. Guess no one's been here since I left some time ago," he mused as he pushed open the heavy wooden door. "Guess I'll have me a few peaceful days here," he thought. "No damn Ve'hoe, white men, about, and I'll worry about the bear tomorrow."

Sinking into what passed for a chair he had made from hewed logs strapped together with leather ties, Johnny O'Shaughnessy Redfeather settled back with a bottle of laudanum, hoping to find a modicum of peace within himself.

5
Redfeather's Return

Nine days later Johnny Redfeather strolled into Milly's Green River Saloon a few minutes after she opened at noon. The dining area was sparsely populated, and the saloon had yet to attract its usual mix of early drinkers. He stopped at the bar just as Milly came around the corner from the back room.

"Well, Johnny Redfeather, aren't you a nice surprise! Didn't think I'd see or hear from you again for quite a while after what we all heard happened up at Reiser. Sheriff says it was downright terrible. I sure am sorry, Johnny. Shooting up my saloon is one thing, but attacking women and children is another thing entirely. Don't see how any man could do something like that."

"Well, Milly, maybe you just don't understand what white men can do. Some of them, they get around Indians, they become one-hundred percent evil. No limit at all."

"Well, I knew Tompkin was rough, and that bastard O'Sullivan from the railroad was overall dirty as a burnt log, especially when he was drunk, but that attack was worse than almost anything I ever heard. Well, except maybe Sand Creek back in sixty-four."

"Well, Milly, Reiser Canyon was just another Sand Creek. Sheriff tried to stop it, I guess, got a posse up there all right, but like Running Bear said, just too late. Only a few left now. And they've already started moving on. Can't say exactly where. Running Bear has buried most of his braves. Not many of them left either."

"Well, like I said, I sure am sorry. Say, now that you're here, Courtney's upstairs and she's got some news you had better learn about. I'll send Snuffy up to fetch her if you want."

"Yeah, you do that. And how is that little rascal? I haven't seen her in some time now. She still causing all kinds of trouble around here? And how's Old Willie? I got to talk to him too. Actually, both of them together."

"Johnny, Snuffy is just fine, but Old Willie's dead. Died here last Monday night."

"What? Dead! Old Willie is dead?"

"Yeah. Just a week ago today. He was playing that old beat-up guitar over in his corner, trying I guess to keep up with whatever tune he thought Charlie was banging on the piano, when he suddenly died sitting in his chair. He keeled over, dropped his guitar. And that was all. We buried him next morning out back. Put up a little marker for him. Poor old guy. Just rode into town one day in that old wagon of his, nobody knows from where."

"I'll be all go to hell! Too late. God-damnit! Me and the Sheriff. Both too late when it really matters. How'd Snuffy take it? She all right?"

"Yeah, I guess so now, but at first she took it really hard. Some of my ladies sort of helping her out, trying, you know, to comfort her. She and Old Willie spent lots of time together ever since he arrived back last July. Anytime you weren't around, she'd be with Old Willie, helping him chop wood, pretending to listen to his old guitar. Asking him questions about what he called 'black folks' music' he claimed he learned to play down in Louisiana before the war. He took a likin' to Snuffy all right, even asked me once about where she come from. I told him 'Never you mind 'bout Snuffy, you just leave that little kid alone. She doesn't need to know anything more than what she does right now.' He wasn't really happy with that, but he never asked me again. I guess he had no one else in his life, but he sure was fond of her."

"Milly, Old Willie was Snuffy's father. Don't tell me you never suspected that."

"Her father? What? Johnny, are you sure about that?"

"Yeah, I'm sure. You ever look at her face underneath all that hair? She's got Willie's eyes all right. You look close you'll see that."

"Well, I never looked that closely, but when they were together I did think once or twice that I saw some resemblance between them. And Willie wanted to know who her mama was. Yeah, I had my suspicions, and I often wondered why he asked me that."

"What about her Mama? You know her?"

"Yeah, I knew her. Name was Amanda, all she ever told me. She arrived here three-months pregnant about fourteen years ago. Said she had been working for the railroad east of here, Rock Springs I think. She said she just had to leave. Didn't say why, so I didn't ask. I figured from her dark complexion and long black hair she was from somewhere in Mexico. She worked here about a year all told, died about six months after her daughter was born. She once asked me never to tell anyone around here where she came from. I promised her that, and so I never told Snuffy or Willie what I knew about her. Oh, and since I'm telling you all this, you should know that Snuffy's real name is also Amanda. Her mama named her that the minute she knew her baby was a girl."

"Willie never knew any of this, right? Never knew about Amanda?"

"Right. He said once or twice that Snuffy reminded him of a woman he lived with for a spell, but since I never told him what I knew about Amanda he never knew for sure who the kid's mother was. He just said he and the woman split up, but nothing more. I never knew when or where, and I didn't ask. I just figured, like Amanda's story, Willie's wasn't much of my business. He sat outside in the warm weather, sort of played his guitar, chopped wood for the stoves, slept in a tiny room in the back in winter or when he wandered back here from wherever he went in that old buggy. Like you in a way. Just comes and goes as he pleases, mysterious like."

"So Snuffy knows nothing about her parents. Nothing!"

"Right. Why?"

"Milly, listen now. I got to talk to Snuffy. She has to know about her and Willie, and a whole lot more. It's time. I'm figuring on taking her to Eagle Canyon. We can ride out together tomorrow. Be back before dark. I promise."

"Well, guess I can trust you all right. Snuffy's out back, sitting by herself. Ever since Old Willie died she's been pretending to play his guitar, trying to make some tunes. Seems that's all she's got left of him now. I'll be right back."

Milly walked behind the bar and poured out a generous shot of whiskey.

"Here, Johnny. This one's on me and Frank."

"Thanks, Milly. I'll wait here."

Just as Redfeather downed his whiskey, a piercing voice from the top of the staircase leading to the upper rooms shattered the calm. "Johnny Redfeather, you lousy Indian rascal, where the hell you been?

You have not been here in a month, and I got news you need to hear. Get your red ass up here! Now!"

Redfeather immediately reached behind the bar for the whiskey bottle and poured himself a second shot, then turned toward the stairs and looked up. "Why if it isn't the quiet one! Darla dear, how are you? Nice to hear from you again."

"Come on up here! Now! Don't 'quiet one' me! I am not interested in your clever tongue. You and me got something big to talk about, and it can't wait either!"

"Darla dear, I'm waiting on Snuffy. Soon as we've talked for a few minutes, I'll come up to your room. But don't go screaming at me. I've had business to tend to up at Reiser Canyon, as I am sure you can understand. Now be nice and I'll be there in a few minutes. Go get some more beauty rest. That always makes you look better, and calms you down. And I figure since I saw you last you probably need help in both of them categories."

"I don't need help in any category, as you call it, and you know it! I had all the help I needed on New Year's Eve, as you may recall. Snuffy's got no news you need to know. I do. Never mind that little monster. Now get on up here!"

"In a minute, Darla. Promise."

Redfeather turned to see Milly and Snuffy shuffling slowly toward him. Snuffy looked even more unkempt than he had remembered her. Her long, shaggy hair nearly covered her entire face, and Johnny guessed she had not changed her clothes since Willie died. When she said "Hi, Johnny," all the sassiness that Redfeather remembered in her voice was gone.

"Snuffy, very sorry about Old Willie. I was planning on us all taking a little ride out to Eagle Canyon together. Now it's just you and me. Tomorrow we can both ride on my horse. Won't take but a few hours, but it's important that we talk. Especially now that Old Willie's gone. There's some stuff you got to know now. Ya hear? Nine o'clock tomorrow morning. We'll ride with the sun. Now I got to see about Darla upstairs. Seems she got some news that I have to hear. That right, Milly?"

"Yeah, it sure is. Now get on up there, go on. Snuffy, you come with me now. Think I'll snip some of them curly locks, and it's time you had a bath and some clean clothes. And don't argue with me this time. You got to move on now. I'll see you in a minute in the back room. Go on, git!"

Snuffy turned, looked back at Redfeather, and, choking back tears, walked toward the back of the saloon. "Seeing as how you're taking Snuffy for a ride tomorrow, seems you might as well stay here tonight. Sheriff might be coming in. Probably be glad to see you. Supper at six if you're interested. See you then."

"Sure, depending on how much of me is left after talking with Miss Courtney Dillard." Redfeather walked slowly toward the stairs at the far end of the saloon. "Okay, Darla, I'm coming up. At your service."

Courtney Dillard, scowling, hands on hips, wearing a loosely fitting blue robe that barely concealed her large breasts, her dark curly hair hanging loosely over her shoulders, met Redfeather at the top of the stairs. "What do you mean running out on me? You haven't been here steady for most of a month now."

"Darla, listen to me, will you? I...."

"And don't come in here talking like you own this saloon and calling me Darla. My name's Courtney. Or do I have to remind you of that every time I see you now?"

"Darla, er Courtney, like I told Milly I've been with Running Bear and what's left of his tribe up in Reiser Canyon. Couldn't wait. Try to understand that."

"Yeah, well, I got something else that can't wait either. Now come into my room."

Courtney led Redfeather into her room down at the far end of the hallway, then shut the door and sat down on her bed. "You lousy red rascal, listen to me really good. You and me are gonna have a child. Way I figure it, looking at the calendar, I got pregnant New Year's Eve, and that makes you the father. Hadn't been anyone else with me in my bed between that night and when my bleeding should have come, so it figures that makes you the daddy. You gonna have another little Indian brave. Isn't that sweet? Now, what you gonna do about that? And you better have the answer I'm looking for!"

Johnny Redfeather collapsed into the chair at the foot of Courtney's bed. "Well I'll be all go to hell," he mumbled. "That sure wasn't what I expected you to tell me. You sure that's my kid in that belly of yours?"

"Yes, I told you how I know. No question about it. Your little Indian in there, Papa Redfeather. Yours! Seems now you got to make some plans. I'm not looking to raise a baby in this god-damn stinking saloon. Nothing but filthy drunks stuffing' dollar bills down our dresses, grabbing our tits, climbing all over us, then calling us 'filthy whores' till they come back two nights later begging for more. You want your little Indian kid in a place like this? Have him turn out like that Snuffy monster down there? That what you want?"

"Miss Darla, I got no god-damn idea what I want right now! None! I never figured on having a kid. This isn't a place for Indians any more, way white people are stealing Indian land, killing buffalo and everything Indians care about. Hell, killing Indians! Why would I want a new Indian baby now?"

"I can't answer that, Johnny. For sure not now. But you got to figure things out in a hurry, cause this kid's growing and I'm not planning on spending the next six months entertaining Milly's filthy, drunken 'patrons' as she calls them. I'm done with that. Milly and I will have to talk, but I got to feed myself and this baby. And you got to help me do that, Daddy Redfeather! You understand what I'm telling you?"

"Yeah, I guess I understand some of that. But right now I got to see about that 'little monster' as you call her. Snuffy and I got to ride out to Eagle Canyon in the morning. I got some serious talking to do with her, too, and that can't wait either."

"Well, that's fine. She's all broken up since Old Willie died last week. Maybe you can help her. But don't you dare run off on me again, you hear?"

"Yes, Miss Darla. I hear."

"Courtney. Mama Courtney Dillard!"

6
Eagle Canyon

At exactly nine o'clock the next morning, Johnny Redfeather began guiding his horse slowly toward Eagle Canyon, about six miles northwest of town. Snuffy, whom Redfeather liked to call his "lieutenant," sat cradled in his left arm on the saddle in front of him.

"Johnny," Snuffy asked just as they left Milly's Saloon, "what's this about anyway? Why we going out to this canyon?"

"Never you mind now. Wait 'till we get there. Then you'll begin to understand. Just hush for now."

After a leisurely ride, during which neither spoke another word, they arrived at the north rim of the canyon. A gentle breeze, roaming east to west, caressed the leaves of dozens of tall cottonwood trees rising from broad ridges on the canyon's western wall. The early summer sun, still fairly low on the horizon, cast ten thousand shadows from the swaying leaves pirouetting on the west side of the canyon. As his horse approached the gently sloping rim, Redfeather halted. "Snuffy, this is Eagle Canyon. You won't find a more beautiful place anywhere in these mountains and canyons than right here. It's also sacred to Indian people, especially Cheyenne, like Running Bear's tribe, but also other tribes, including the Apache. That's part of what I brought you up here to learn about. Now let's get down off this horse and sit a spell, here at this entrance. Come on."

Redfeather dismounted, then lifted Snuffy off the saddle and let her down, but not before hugging her close to him. "Katsee, little girl," he said softly. He tethered his horse, then he and Snuffy walked a few yards down toward the sloping entrance to the huge canyon. With the sun warming their backs, they sat down on the grass and gazed into the canyon's immense depth. After a few minutes, as he sensed Snuffy getting restless, Redfeather cleared his throat, and turned toward her.

"Now, Snuffy, Otahe! Listen to me. You and I are mixed up in similar ways. My father was an Irishman, name O'Shaughnessy. I can't remember anymore the last time I saw him. But growing up my mama insisted he was my papa, so I got to take her word. Now my mama was Indian, she said Timucua, that's down Florida way, but she said that way back she was sure she was Cheyenne. She told me that her mama, my gramma, was the daughter of a chief, and I think she and my grandpa were both Cheyenne from out here somewhere. Maybe some Apache in their blood, maybe not. Doesn't matter all that much now. How they all got to Florida I have no idea, but that doesn't make any difference now either. I just tell people, like Sheriff Talbot, that I'm part Cheyenne, and I see no reason to complicate that anymore. White people, Ve'ho'e, call me 'half-breed,' cause I'm half Indian and some part Irish, but I hate that term, and so I just think of myself as Cheyenne Indian. Nothing more than that is necessary."

Snuffy looked at Redfeather in bewilderment. "Why you telling' me all this? I've never worried about any of this. Aren't you just Johnny Redfeather?"

"Yeah, that's right, I'm just Johnny Redfeather, but here's where you come in. Now, Otahe, listen carefully. He'kotoo'estse, sit still, calm down. I know you don't know anything about your parents, and Milly promised your mama not to tell anyone about her child, but now you got to know. First, Old Willie was your father."

"What? Old Willie? He was my father? Says who? How do you know that?"

"Well, I gather you never suspected that, but it's true. All I had to do was look at your eyes really close once, maybe late last summer, and I could see Old Willie's eyes in yours sure as damnation. He once asked Milly about you, said you reminded him of a Mexican woman he said he once lived with several years ago, but Milly kept her promise to your mama and never told Willie about her or where she and you came from. But Willie always believed you were his child, which is why he took such a strong liking to you and wanted to spend time with you when he was back at Milly's."

"Johnny, if this is true, why didn't Willie ever tell me? All that time I could have known he was my pa, and I didn't! That's not right!"

"Well, yeah, I guess maybe you're right about that. But like I said,

Milly kept your mama's promise to keep your story secret. Still, I'm sure Willie died believing he had found his Nahtse, daughter, though he never knew for certain what happened to the woman he was living with. Something drove them apart before you were born, so he just assumed he'd never see his child again. Until he somehow got to Milly's in that ragged old buggy. And once he saw you he would do anything to convince Milly to let him stay around just so's he could be with you as much as possible. Play that no-good guitar, chop wood, anything just to stay wherever you were."

As Redfeather finished talking, Snuffy hung her head between her knees, and began sobbing. "Johnny, why didn't he tell me what he believed? Why? I deserved to know he was my pa."

"Because he didn't know for sure, and because Milly told him to just leave you alone about where you came from. It was your mama's wish that Milly say nothing about you to anybody, even yourself. Maybe your mama was embarrassed because she wasn't with your father any more, or there was something about her and him she didn't want anybody to know. I can't rightly say, but it doesn't matter now. Too late, except for what else you need to know now about your ma."

Snuffy raised her head and scanned the rim of the canyon. "Those trees are sure pretty," she murmured, becoming slowly aware now of the canyon's beauty surrounding her, despite the grief she could barely understand. She wiped her eyes on her sleeve, then turned to Redfeather. "So, what about my mama you got to tell me?"

Redfeather looked deep into the canyon looming before him. "Milly never quite understood this, but one look at your cheek bones and your skin, and any fool can see your mama was Indian. Don't know what tribe, or nation, but Indian for sure. Maybe Apache. Like me maybe way back, or even maybe Comanche or Kickapoo from Mexico. Can't say for sure, but you're Indian all right. White people will call you a 'half-breed,' which isn't nice, but you got to know you are all Indian on your mama's side, and you got to learn to be proud of that. And don't let anybody ever take that from you or say you're worth nothing because you're Indian. Never! Like the Cheyenne say, He'konetanohtse, be strong!"

Snuffy glared at Redfeather. "So you're telling me I'm just like you? How do you know that? If this is so, where's this mama of mine? Why haven't I ever known about her either?"

"Indians know Indians when they see one, even if they're mixed.

Milly only says your mama died about six months after you were born. She arrived in Green River, alone Milly says, and asked for help. Milly saw she was going to have a child, so she gave her room and board in exchange for working at the saloon, cooking or cleaning. Nothing else! She went out walking one night, caught a chill, died some days later of a terrible fever. Doc Johnson couldn't save her. So Milly and the other women raised you, or tried to. You know the rest, and now you know the beginning, though not all of it or exactly where your mama and papa came from. But that doesn't matter now. It's just the knowing that matters. And this all is Hetomestotse, the truth."

Snuffy drew her knees to her chest, and began sobbing. After a few minutes, Redfeather touched her shoulder, but she pulled away. "So my mother was an Indian? And I'm never gonna know who she was or where she came from! What am I supposed to do with hearing all this from you? Why can't I have a mama and a papa like the other children I see in town? Why do I have to be different? Why can't I live in a house somewhere in town, not that dirty, smelly saloon where everybody's always yelling at me? My daddy was there and nobody ever told me that! I could've known I was with my pa! But I never did! And why we at this damn canyon? Why not just you and Milly tell me all this back at the saloon?"

Redfeather reached for Snuffy's shoulder, and again she pulled back. "And don't touch me!" she screamed and, sobbing and shaking, pressed her face into her knees.

"Snuffy, listen to me, please. First off, I can't answer all your questions. Like I said, your mama asked Milly never to talk about her or your daddy. All I know is what I can do for you now, and that starts with your name. It's Amanda, like your mother's. That's a part of your mother you will always have. I know you like Snuffy, and I know why, because I let you chew some of my snuff, but that's not right, and that's got to stop. Now! That's no damn good for an Indian girl. From now on, I want to try to be more like a father for you. Courtney tells me I'm the father of her child that's coming, so I need practice. That sound all right with you, Amanda?"

Snuffy brushed wet curls from her face and looked up at Redfeather. "Those Indian tears you're crying?" he asked. "They sure look Indian to me."

"Maybe. I can't see 'em." Still sobbing, she turned away and gazed into the canyon below them. "You still haven't told me why we're here. Maybe that'd be one thing I could understand today."

"Because this is Eagle Canyon, and for all time this place has been sacred to Indians, Cheyenne mostly, but other tribes too, including Apache. I brought Sheriff Talbot out here after Tompkin's men killed Running Bear's people up in Reiser Canyon. I told him no white man could ever destroy this canyon, even though they might try, just like they're trying to destroy everything Indians got out here. And now you got to know this canyon is part of who you are. Always will be, just like it's part of who I am, and always will be. Nothing will ever change that."

"And I'm supposed to do what now, knowing all this?" Snuffy snapped through her tears.

"Can't say for sure just yet. Maybe you'll find out later. Like I said, it's knowing the truth, Hetomestotse, that matters now. When the time comes for you to do something with this knowledge, you'll know. And I trust you'll do what's right. Now, let's get back to town. I got to ride out to Reiser Canyon a few more times before Running Bear leaves for good."

"You gonna tell Milly all this? Sheriff Talbot? Anyone else?"

"Milly doesn't need to know more just yet. Maybe later, but leave that to me. Sheriff, maybe. I'll decide that. You just keep this to yourself for the time being. Now one more thing I got to do. Just stay there, and keep your head up. I'll kneel behind you. Won't take but a few minutes."

"What you fixing on doing now?"

"Just relax. I see Milly didn't cut your hair like she said she would."

"Yeah, I got real mad yesterday when she said she wanted to do that. So she gave up. She said I couldn't hardly see through so much hair, but I told her I liked it."

"Good! Now just hold steady." Redfeather reached into his shirt pocket and pulled out a comb and some thin leather laces. "You could maybe start to wear your hair Indian style." He began combing and separating her hair into two strands, then tied them with the leather strips into two long braids. "There, now that looks better. See how you like that for a while. Don't have to keep it that way if you don't want to, but I think your mama would have approved. Take a look when we get back to Milly's. Now, Noheto, we got to go."

Snuffy pulled at her braids, then turned to Redfeather. "Feels funny, almost like all my hair is gone."

"It's all still there, just in different places. And now you can see better!"

"Yeah, I guess so. Johnny, one more thing. Where do you go when you're not around Milly's? She and some of the girls were wondering 'bout that some nights ago, right after Willie died."

"Don't worry your little head about that. I got places, including what's left of Running Bear's camp, though that's about to end. But I'm all right. Never you mind. Now, Noheto, let's go." They walked back to Redfeather's horse, and he lifted her onto his saddle. "Hang on, we'll ride faster now."

After Redfeather mounted, Snuffy turned around. "Johnny, who I'm supposed to be from now on? Amanda? Snuffy?"

"You choose. Your name is yours, not mine. I told Milly that Old Willie was your father, and she was surprised though I think she suspected that for some time. So for sure she's told everyone at the saloon, and she knows your real name."

"I like my mama's name. Amanda. Seems real pretty."

"Yes, Amanda, it sure is."

"You call me Amanda, but maybe for now at Milly's I'll still be Snuffy. That all right with you?"

"Yes, Amanda, it sure is. Whatever you decide is fine with me."

Redfeather gazed once more into the enchanting depths of Eagle Canyon, then directed his horse toward Green River. Neither he nor Amanda spoke as they rode. Redfeather knew that although most of the women at Milly's called Amanda a "little monster" because she seemed absolutely ungovernable, he believed now that her strong will would protect her against whatever obstacles the town or the indifferent wilderness surrounding them would hurl at her.

Once outside Milly's Saloon, Redfeather stopped, then lifted Amanda off his horse. "Now you listen to me, Amanda. Anyone in there asks you about this ride and our talk, you just tell them we went to look at a canyon. No need to say anything more about today. And when you see Darla, tell her I'll be coming by to see her soon. And I'll come by to check on you too. And don't forget what I told you about Eagle Canyon. Understand?"

"Yes," Amanda replied softly. "I understand. Thanks, Johnny," and she put her arms around his neck and kissed his cheek. "Guess I'll get on inside. See how Milly and Frank like my Indian hair."

"Tell them Johnny Redfeather said it's beautiful."

7
Colonel William Swanson

Saturday nights at Milly's Green River Saloon were usually crowded, lively, and hectic, and this Saturday was no exception. Marilee, Roxy, and the other young women who served the crowded tables scattered around the dining area shuffled plates of food from the kitchen and glasses of whiskey and beer from the bar to their waiting customers. At the bar Frank filled whiskey orders as fast as he could, and his cook, Sam, was nearly overwhelmed preparing large orders of meat and potatoes on the two wood-burning stoves in the back room. His occasionally nasty curses at one of the impatient waitresses asking when her order would be done prompted Milly to remind him that hers was a "sophisticated saloon, not a low-down joint like Hal's up the street," and that "he had better mind his tongue if he expected to be working here another night." Charley, the remaining member of the Charley-Willie duo, banged away at his piano creating melodies only he could comprehend.

Sheriff Jim Talbot and Butch Grogan entered around seven o'clock, just as Milly had asked. She greeted them as they entered and escorted them to a table she had told Marilee to reserve for them. "Why Sheriff, you are prompt! Deputy Grogan, nice to see you again. I've been wondering when I might see you two in here again on a Saturday night. Been a while."

"Well, Milly, hasn't been all that long. Couple weeks maybe," Talbot remarked as he and Grogan pulled back chairs at a small table and sat down. Talbot realized immediately that something was missing from the countless Saturday nights he had spent at Milly's, enjoying himself while ensuring that her patrons, especially the heavy drinkers, most of whom he knew all too well, behaved themselves. "Say Milly, where's Old Willie? I hear whatever Charlie has got rolling around in his head, but Willie's not sitting next to him on his chair. He sick or something?"

Milly lowered her head, took a deep breath. She recalled how much Sheriff Talbot had enjoyed listening to Old Willie's strumming, even if neither he nor anyone else in the saloon could identity what he played as "music." Just noise, Talbot once remarked; but enjoyable noise, he would add.

"Sheriff, Old Willie is dead. Died the last Monday in April. You weren't here, I know. Grogan wasn't either. I figured you'd be here tonight, seeing' as how I asked you to come by. Sorry to have to be the one to tell you this. He died peacefully, that's for sure. Just fell over in his chair, and that was that. Wish I could send his guitar after him. We just left it leaning against a tree by his grave out back. Maybe his ghost will come take it, maybe make some real music with it."

Before either Talbot or Grogan could speak, Marilee arrived with two whiskeys and two glasses of beer. She smiled at them as she laid the drinks on the table. "Here you go Sheriff, just what you and Butch need on a Saturday night. You let me know if you need another round. I'll be here the whole night."

"Butch and I thank you, Marilee. That's real nice of you. How you been?"

"Well, in general, or since you been in here? Which is it?"

"I didn't know there was a difference. Guess in general would do for now."

"In general, all right I guess. Not much new around here. Never is. After I saw you in here back in April I was hoping I'd see you again sooner. Either here or elsewhere in town. Where you been hiding yourself?"

At Marilee's question, Milly waved at Talbot and Grogan and walked away. "See you around, Sheriff," she remarked as she headed back toward the bar.

Talbot turned toward Marilee, who was leaning on the edge of the table, her other hand parked on her hip. "Not hiding, Marilee. Butch and I been out talking to Jesse Smith about his herd, out at Tompkin's old place. Trying to reach some agreement about where he can drive his herd this winter, what creeks he can use for water, making sure he knows about Indians' hunting grounds, whatever is left of treaties out here. Went up to Reiser Canyon once, saw Redfeather there with Running Bear. I wasn't exactly welcomed, so I didn't stay long. Been back at my cabin at Brown's Wash most nights, just trying to get used to Abigail's not being there. Still hard to do even after so many months, harder than I thought it would be."

At Talbot's mention of his deceased wife, Marilee stiffened, straightened her torso and, as she walked away from Talbot's table, muttered to herself, "Man's locked himself up, thrown away the key."

Talbot sat down and placed his Stetson on the table. Grogan sipped his whiskey, then turned to him. "Sheriff, I remember from last New Year's Day up at your office how bad you're hurt inside, and I'm sure it's nothing I've ever experienced, at least not yet. But diamonds to dollars that pretty young woman sure has got an eye for you. Seems might be worth some of your time, take your mind off Abigail, all that's happened here recently. Can't reclaim any of what's gone, and you got to stop blaming yourself for what happened at Reiser Canyon. A little bit of comfort from that sweet young lady might be really helpful right now."

"Butch, you may be right. It's just that...." As Talbot's voice faded, a tall, slender man wearing a black, wide-brimmed Stetson, white cotton shirt, red leather vest with a gold watch chain dangling from a pocket, matching red cotton scarf, dark denim jeans, black leather boots, a rifle case slung over his right shoulder, and carrying two large suitcases approached his table and extended his right hand.

"Excuse me, sir. Lady at the bar tells me you're the Sheriff here in Green River and hereabouts. Name's William Swanson, retired Colonel, United States Army. We met briefly in Georgia during the war. I'm very pleased to renew your acquaintance, and to learn that the local sheriff is a man I've met before."

"Swanson! Colonel William Swanson! What? Well I'll be damned! What a surprise seeing you in Green River!" Talbot exclaimed loudly as he rose and shook Swanson's hand vigorously. "You're about the last man I ever expected to see way out here. My God, what a surprise! Can't believe this! So the stories I've heard about your death are obviously wrong! What, how . . . ? Damn but this doesn't seem possible!"

"Well, Sheriff, believe it," Swanson replied and laughed loudly. "I did not know that rumors of my death were circulating after the war. That's a grim surprise, I must say. Maybe we can talk about that nonsense later. But anyway, I just got into town, and thought I'd get some food and a beer, maybe have a whiskey too. That's a hard, dusty ride by wagon from the end of the railroad."

"Don't I know that. Oh, Colonel, this young man is my deputy,

Butch Grogan," Talbot said as Grogan stood and shook Swanson's hand. "Butch, this gentleman is Colonel William Swanson. Remember the story I told you about Johnny freeing some Union forces? Well, they were Colonel Swanson's men."

"What? You knew Johnny Redfeather? What a surprise. Well, I am sure glad to meet you."

"Much obliged, I am sure. And yes, you might say I knew Johnny Redfeather. We had quite an experience together."

"Butch, we knew each other in the war in Georgia, late sixty-four and some time in sixty-five. That about right, Colonel?"

"Yes, that sounds right," Swanson added. "We spent some time together, not much, but enough that I am very pleased to meet you again. I recall you as a real Virginia gentleman, one of a small number of officers I really respected. Not out for Southern blood at the end. Just wanted to end all those awful days that are now best forgotten."

"Oh, that's truly kind of you, Colonel. Well, by all means, have a seat," Talbot said, and pulled over a third chair as he and Grogan sat down. "Put your cases down and sit a while. What brings you to Green River? Oh Butch, could you get us three beers right away?"

Grogan stood up. "Oh for sure, Sheriff. I'll go ask Milly for three more. Be right back."

"Thank you, Butch."

Swanson turned to Talbot. "I must say meeting somebody I know right away in a strange place sure can be comforting. You're looking well, Jim. You seem to have survived all right. Lot better than many men I remember."

"Well, mostly all right I guess. Came west to start over, forget what I left behind. Became sheriff in July last year, been trying to keep peace between Indians and cattle folks and the railroad. Pretty violent at times, especially lately. But enough about me. What the hell brings you to Green River?"

"Well, been working on the Union Pacific since shortly after the war ended. Always moving west you know, just like hundreds, maybe thousands more these days. I figured once I got to a town I'd break off for a spell, maybe do a little hunting up in these mountains now that it's warmer and nights are longer. Heard about the canyons too. Folks say they're just magnificent. Right now I'm just looking to meet some people, find a room. Never know, might even consider settling down if it suits me, especially now that I know the sheriff in town. I figure he can keep me out of trouble if anyone can! Say, how's the food here? I'm damn hungry."

"Well," Talbot added, "Food's pretty good here. Beer and whiskey are better. Just don't tell Milly I said that."

"Ha, I sure won't. Yeah, beer sounds damn good right now."

Just then Butch returned with three glasses of beer. "Mr. Swanson, Sheriff, here you go."

"Thank you, Butch," Talbot said. "Colonel William Swanson, a true survivor, here's to your happy return from the rumors of your death. Welcome to Green River!" Sheriff Talbot raised his glass and Grogan and Swanson joined him. "Thank you, Jim and Butch," Swanson replied. "And here's to perhaps many happy days in Green River."

The men drank heartily, then placed their glasses on the table. "Bill," Talbot began, "you knew a Doctor Mark Johnson in the war, right?"

"Damn straight I did! Also down in Georgia, especially near the end. Good man. I recall that he once told me that when the war ended he was determined to travel west, like you just to get away. He was a fine physician. I recall that he saved many lives, always respected the wounded men he treated even though he hated what they were doing. He was what I'd call a man dedicated to peace. Can't say I knew many more men like him. Kind, selfless. I would have liked to see him after the war ended, but I have no idea where he went after he left Georgia in sixty-five."

"Well, you will be very surprised to know that Doctor Mark Johnson is also here in Green River. Got here before I did, set up a practice serving both whites and Indians. He has a small office in town, and his own place a few miles north of here. He comes in here fairly often, so if you return to Milly's for grub and beer you will probably see him. I am sure he would be thrilled to see you again."

"Well I'll be damned! I get off a dusty stage coach out here in the wilds of Dakota Territory and lo and behold here are two of my former acquaintances from the Civil War! If that doesn't just beat all!"

"Well, here's another surprise, saving the best for last. Johnny Redfeather is in the area around Green River."

"What? Redfeather? Redfeather? Johnny Redfeather? You can't be serious! This all is not possible! What the hell is he doing here? How did he get here, for heaven's sake?"

"Well, I don't know all the details, but as best I know, after escaping with you from that prison in Georgia he came north looking for his mother's Cheyenne people. Once he got here, I think last spring, he spent some time with Running Bear's tribe up in Reiser Canyon, and also, unfortunately, too much time in saloons around town. But last September, after a raid on Milly's here by a bunch of drunken herders and railroad men, Johnny saved this place, and me, almost single-handedly. Never seen anything like what he did. Then after all the shooting stopped Doc Johnson told us the story of your escape."

"Oh how I'd love to see Johnny Redfeather again! He's the sole reason I am still alive. God bless that man! After traveling two days through those awful swamps and the terrible snakes—god-damn but they terrified me!—and we got back to my regiment, Johnny left, said he was bound for the mountains up north as by then both the Rebel and Yankee armies were after his hide. Haven't seen him since. I assumed he was dead, that soldiers from either side finally got him. Lord knows what either would have done to that man. By the end of the war, everybody in Georgia hated him, wanted his scalp, you might say."

"Yeah, that's what Doc said. A hunted man. Anyway, he's in here once in a while. Seems nearly everyone in town stops here. So once you get settled in, come back and you're sure to find Johnny eventually. He's got a girlfriend here who's expecting his child, so he's likely to be here more often than usual now."

"Johnny Redfeather a father! Now that's something I never figured to hear. By the way, Jim, what's this about rumors of my death? I mean me dead! Hell no man! I'm sitting here drinking beer and whiskey with you and your deputy! Dead's the last thing I am. Where the devil you all get that idea?

"Well, one day last summer, before I really knew Johnny well, he came running up the street yelling at me that he had heard you were dead. Said he'd heard from some drunk ex-soldier in Hal's Saloon up the street that you died in Georgia near the end of the war. Something about a crazy rebel soldier shooting after everyone thought there was a cease-fire somewhere. Made Johnny raging mad. But obviously that report was wrong. Johnny will sure be glad to hear you are very much alive, and in Green River too!"

"Well, speaking of dead, I was sure Johnny was dead by now. Figured if the soldiers didn't get him before the war ended one of them terrible snakes in Georgia sure would. That man would tangle with any wild animal, even those damned cottonmouths."

"Yeah, that sounds like Johnny all right," added Grogan. "Sheriff Talbot has been telling me stories about him, how he shoots cross-fire, dead-on every time. Fast as lightning and twice as deadly. Afraid of no man, drunk or sober."

"Yup, that's Redfeather all right. Now you got to tell me where I can find him. Can't believe he's alive, and in these parts."

Sheriff Talbot laughed. "Well, that's always a bit of a mystery around here. Sometimes Johnny will be in here, seeing a young lady named Darla, as he calls her, and sometimes up in Reiser Canyon near what's left of an Indian encampment. Band of Cheyenne under Chief Running Bear was attacked by a gang led by this rancher named Tompkin. Killed damn near everyone up there, children too, except the Chief and a few braves and some women. Well, Johnny was up there for a while right afterwards, helping Running Bear as best he could. I'd guess Running Bear won't be there for long. So I don't know exactly where Johnny is, though maybe he's in a cabin somewhere up in these mountains. Anywhere that isn't Reiser Canyon."

As Talbot finished speaking Roxy and Marilee walked up to their table. "Well, Sheriff," Roxy said, "who's your handsome friend here?"

"Marilee, and Roxy, this is Colonel William Swanson, Johnny Redfeather's friend who he thought had died in the war. But he's come back from the grave!"

"My goodness, won't Johnny be surprised!" Marilee said. "Welcome to Green River, Colonel Swanson. Sure am glad you're here."

"You planning to stay a while?" asked Roxy.

"Well, I just might. You're all making me feel really welcome, I must say. Sheriff tells me Johnny Redfeather is somewhere out here. That's reason enough to stay a while. What a damn good surprise that would be, seeing Johnny again. Say, how about I buy a round of your finest whiskey?"

"Why sure," responded Marilee. "Coming right up. I'll be right back."

"Colonel Swanson, you need anything else in here tonight, just come looking for me," Roxy remarked. "This place is getting crowded now, but you can find me sure enough. I'll be here all night," Roxy added as she turned back toward the bar.

"Why, I'll remember that. Much obliged, I'm sure."

Marilee returned a few minutes later with three full whiskey glasses and set them down on the table. "This here's our best whiskey, so everyone insists. Hope you like it," Marilee said. "Jim, glad you're here. Maybe we'll find a few minutes to talk tonight. Now I got to get back to serving tables. Duty, you know, as you are always reminding me."

"Right! Yes. Well, thank you, Marilee. Yes, long as this place stays peaceful tonight, I'm sure we can find a few minutes to talk. See you around," Talbot said, and smiled at Marilee.

"This place always so friendly?" Swanson asked. "Or just on Saturday nights?"

"Nah, Milly's place is generally friendly, wouldn't you say Sheriff?" Grogan remarked.

"Yeah, I'd agree," said Talbot. "Mostly. Here's to you, Colonel William Swanson! My God! Welcome to Green River. Thanks for the whiskey."

"You're most welcome!"

Talbot sipped his whiskey, then scanned the saloon's large interior, looking for any of the usual troublemakers he might recognize. Not seeing any suspects at the moment, he looked toward the bar and spotted Marilee wiping some glasses. He finished his whiskey, then turned to Swanson and Grogan.

"If you two gentlemen will excuse me for a moment I'll wander over to the bar and speak with Miss Marilee for a bit. Butch, you'll know where to find me. I'll probably bunk down at my office tonight, just so you know where I'll be later. Doesn't look like too much trouble tonight, but you never know. I'll see you later. Bill, welcome again to Green River. I suspect I'll see you in town again right soon," Talbot said as he stood.

"Well for sure, Jim" replied Swanson. He stood up and shook Talbot's hand. "Now go on over there and talk to that pretty lady. I suspect she's waiting on you. I wouldn't waste time if I were you."

"No, guess I've wasted enough of that already. Goodnight for now."

"Take it easy, Sheriff," Grogan added. "Say Colonel Swanson, how 'bout I get us one more beer? Don't think the Sheriff would mind if I had one more. You up for that?"

"Well, yes I believe I am. Thank you!"

"You're welcome," Grogan said. "I'll be right back."

"Good. I believe I'll just sit here a spell and enjoy this whiskey that

Marilee brought and then that second beer. Maybe order some food. Jim said it isn't too bad. If you need to help the Sheriff, you go right ahead."

"Well, I'll get us that beer and be right back. Think for the moment at least I ought to leave the Sheriff alone. I'll wander over to the bar a little later, see if he wants me for anything."

At a small, nearby table to the left of the saloon's swinging doors, Jake Bulger sat back in his chair. He grinned as he brought his whiskey glass slowly to his lips and took a sip. "So, you're Colonel William Swanson," he muttered. "What a coincidence! And if I'm not mistaken y'all just might lead me to Johnny Redfeather one of these fine spring days. Then I'll get my revenge on both of you. Well, won't be long now, Hank. Next time you walk in here, Mr. Colonel Swanson, is going to be the beginning of the end for you, you slick-talking Yankee bastard. Just you wait! That's one face I'm not about to forget." Bulger gulped the last of his whiskey, turned the glass upside down on the table, left some coins for Roxy, then rose and walked slowly through the swinging doors to where his horse waited, tethered in front of the saloon. He mounted, then began riding quickly toward Jesse Smith's bunkhouse.

§

"So, not much duty tonight, Jim? Must be really nice," Marilee said as she leaned over the bar, looking directly at Talbot's face. She wore a white blouse, open at her neck and several buttons down, and a white, wide-hoop skirt dotted with flowers. "Seems tonight you got time to spend with someone other than Grogan or some drunken card players. Must be really nice." She picked up several whiskey glasses and started rinsing them in a tub of hot water.

"Yes, Marilee, a somewhat peaceful night in here is welcome. But nicer standing here talking to you. How you been?"

"Well, I'm all right I guess. What's it now, nearly three weeks since you been in here? You know, several men have, shall we say, expressed some interest in my company lately. Milly's let on that washing glasses and waiting tables aren't all I was hired on for, you might say. Suppose to be some 'entertainment' for the locals once in a while."

Sheriff Talbot sighed, leaned over the bar, removed a glass from Marilee's hand, and took both her hands in his. "Come over here a minute, please." He walked her over to the nook behind the bar where she had kissed him on New Year's Eve and invited him to stay with her.

"Marilee, don't think I don't know what you're telling me. I know you think I'm stupid, or just too shy, or too much 'Gentleman Jim,' as Abigail used to call me. Well, I'm not stupid, I'm not as shy as maybe you think I am, and I am not hiding behind this damn badge I got pinned on my vest. 'Duty' as you call it is important to me, but I know that life is much more than that, even in a wild place like Green River. Yes, I think about you. Maybe too much, and maybe that's why I'm not here as often as Milly and Frank would like me to be. Yes, I'm lonely, but I'm still mostly lonely for Abigail. It's not even a year since she died, I still don't know for sure who fired that shot, and I still blame myself for bringing her out here. Every time I walk into our cabin out at Brown's Wash I still see her there, hear her voice, feel her touch. Maybe I could be with another woman there, but truthfully, I just don't know. And I don't know when I could do that. And that's the truth. It's not what you wanted me to say, but as I am a gentleman, as Abigail liked to say, it's the truth. Yeah, maybe one day I'll come in here wanting to take you away from this life, but right now I can't promise that."

Marilee grabbed Talbot and pulled him to her breast. She kissed him hard, wrapping her hands around his neck and holding him to her open mouth. "Just so you know what's waiting for you if that day ever comes. I love you, but for now I guess I got to still make my own life here. I wouldn't wait too long if I were you. No girl can wait forever, and there's a lot of money coming into this saloon every damn night."

Talbot kissed her neck, then held her tightly, his hands caressing her back. "So, feel good, Gentleman Jim? Seems you think so. Well, I better go. Milly will be looking for me. You know where I am. Just remember that kiss. I meant it!"

"Yes, Marilee. I know you did."

"Well, at least that's one thing you know now. Some improvement already." She kissed him again, then walked back to the bar to serve several men lined up for whiskey and whatever else they hoped they could buy for the evening. Talbot stood still for a moment, then leaned into the back wall of the nook. "Oh Abigail," he sighed, "are you still there?" He straightened, then walked slowly past the bar and into the boisterous Saturday night of a frontier saloon.

8
Jesse Smith's Bunkhouse

Several days later, after his men had finished eating supper, Jesse Smith approached Jake Bulger at the end of a long table. "Jake, come on outside, sit a spell," Smith said. "Seems you and I should talk a bit."

Moments later they sat at a small table outside the front entrance to the bunkhouse. Smith pulled two cigars from a vest pocket and offered one to Bulger.

"Well, thanks, Jesse, don't mind if I do." Smith leaned over and lighted Bulger's cigar, then his own and sat back in his chair. "So, mind telling me what's eating at you lately? You didn't go out riding with your group last Monday, instead you just prowl around here like a wildcat, avoiding conversation, as well as what you're supposed to be doing on this job, and yelling at people when they ask you to do something. You want out of this job? Want to go do something else? Is that the problem?"

"No, that's not the problem."

"Then tell me what is! I can't afford to have lazy workers in this operation. Back where I come from, you would've been fired days ago. Now what's up?"

"I told you about my brother Hank's death a while back, right? At the prison in Georgia? Had his throat slit, left to die."

"Yeah, you did. So what's that got to do with working here? That was back in sixty-four, right?"

"Yeah, sixty-four. Well, last Saturday night at Milly's in town I saw one of the Yankee prisoners who escaped Lawton and killed Hank. One Colonel William Swanson. He and a half-breed named Johnny Redfeather, who you have heard about from some of the herders here who worked for Tompkin, led the escape. And it's one of them, I'm guessing Redfeather, that slit Hank's throat. And I heard talk in Milly's that Redfeather is in the area. And I got a score to settle for both of them. And that's what's eating at me ever since."

"Listen, Jake, I'm just as Southern as you or anybody else out here. But god-damnit that war is over. You understand? Over! You can't go back and change or fix anything that didn't pan out the way you wanted it to. You think you're the only one who lost people? My best friend's sixteen year old boy got his head shot off by a Yankee cannon. Sixteen! I know you said your brother was younger, but lots of young kids got killed terribly in that war. You're hardly the only one who lost a kid brother."

"Jesse, I know that. But just seeing that fancy-dressed Yankee walk into that saloon and thinking about what he and that god-damn Redfeather did to Hank is eatin' at me way down deep, and I just can't let it go. I can't."

"Well, let me tell you something, Bulger, and don't forget this. I'm trying like hell to run a cattle business out here, and I can't have men refusing to go out with the herds or getting ornery with everybody else in this bunkhouse. Now if you plan to continue working for me on this herd, then you had better start learning to get along with the other men and put that war and everything in it behind you. There's no use trying to change the past. If you have any thoughts of trying to avenge your brother's death, then leave tomorrow morning and don't bother comin' back. You understand me?"

"Yeah, Jesse, I understand you. It's just hard, is all. Just suddenly putting a face on that Swanson name, and then hearin' the sheriff say Redfeather is in the area. It's like Hank's ghost is getting after me all over again."

"Well, tell your brother's ghost that you got herding to do now, and to leave you the hell alone. After what I heard happened at Reiser Canyon I want no trouble around here. So you got a choice: do your work, or leave. Got it?"

"Sure, Jesse, I got it."

"Good. That settles it. Now let's go inside with the other men. Play some cards and have us a whiskey or two."

9
Invitation

Colonel Swanson pushed through the swinging doors of Milly's Saloon about 5:15 on Saturday, May 18. In his clean, blue cotton shirt, brown leather vest and pants, black boots, and Stetson hat he stood out amid the usual crowd lingering around the saloon. Having remembered what Talbot had said after meeting him in the saloon the night he arrived in town—that Saturday nights were the most lively at Milly's—he vowed to return a week later. Talbot had assured him that he would be at Milly's and said he would be happy to introduce Swanson to some of the town's finest citizens. As he had arrived somewhat early he had his choice of tables, and after laying his hat on one to the left of the doors near a small window, he walked toward the bar to order a whiskey and beer.

"Well stranger, nice to see you in here again," a young woman greeted him as he approached her. "Name's Colonel William Swanson, if I'm not mistaken. Where you been hiding? Like a drink or two?"

"Oh, I've been at the Dakota Hotel. Been walking around town, been to the outfitters for some gear I figure I'll need for hunting up in these mountains, inquiring about buying a horse. I'd like to get to see more of this wild country. As for a drink, why, yes, I would. Thank you. Whiskey and beer. And your name is... Sorry I can't remember from last time. I met several people and...."

"Roxy, Roxy Denninger. I served you and Sheriff Talbot the first night you were in here. You'd just got into town I believe, right?"

"Yes, that's right. Sheriff said come by next Saturday and meet some of the folks in here, said he'd probably be here. I think his deputy too."

"Yeah, both are usually here on Saturday nights. Place gets pretty crowded and rowdy sometimes. Sheriff and Grogan keep the peace, mostly. Course sometimes they have to haul a few drunken fools off to the jail up the street, let 'em sober up. But hasn't been too bad since Tompkin and his damn herders are mostly gone now. That was a real bad bunch. Head on back to your table and I'll bring your drinks over. Won't take but a minute."

"Why that's very kind of you. Thanks."

"Sure, don't mention it. Like I said, nice to see you again."

Swanson walked to his table and sat down. Gazing around the large central room of Milly's Saloon he tried to imagine the livelihoods of the motley collection of humanity scattered before him. Having lived the life of a country gentleman in rural New York State before the Civil War, he retained, to the extent he could still afford them, the acquired tastes of a leisurely land owner. His military training at West Point had led to a commission in the Union Army, and in the final two years of the war he had commanded several successful campaigns in the South, especially in Tennessee and Georgia. His father had invested in logging and ship building in Maine and had bequeathed to his son a substantial inheritance. Swanson had returned to New York after the war to settle down and pursue his own agricultural businesses. However, stunned by his father's sudden death in March, 1867, Swanson decided to travel west, partly to relieve his grief and partly to explore the expanding frontier and its possible business opportunities.

"Whiskey and beer, Colonel Swanson," Roxy said as she placed the drinks on the table. "It is Colonel Swanson, right?"

"Why yes, that's right, but just call me William, or Bill. All that colonel stuff was part of the war, and I don't necessarily want any more of that."

"Well, I can understand that all right. And that's quite friendly of you I must say. Not much point in being fancy in this place, though for a saloon I'd say it's the best bet in town, more classy than most you might say. Anyway, that's what Milly is always saying about her place. And I guess she's got a right to say that. It's her place, hers and Frank's."

"I see. And you work here most nights I take it?"

"Well, depends on what you mean by 'work.' Some of us got a kind of double duty around this place. Upstairs, you might say." Roxy glanced at the stairs at the far end of the saloon. "Some nights not so bad, some nights downright awful, if you get my drift."

Swanson smiled, cleared his throat, then looked at Roxy. "Yes, I get your drift. Well, guess maybe I'll keep that in mind. For now, thanks for the whiskey and beer. Oh, and I'll have whatever you got for supper tonight."

"You're sure welcome. Coming right up. I'll bring it over when it's ready. Now if you'll excuse me, I got some tables to wait on. Perhaps I'll see you later tonight."

"Perhaps," Swanson thought as Roxy headed back toward the bar and he slowly sipped his whiskey. The saloon was filling quickly now, with a few genteel, well-dressed married couples, plus several young men and women who fancied themselves among the "better" citizens of Green River—shop owners and their employees, store clerks, bankers, one or two lawyers—mixing with the herders, loggers, and railroad workers who congregated around the bar and shouted their requests for whiskey and room numbers for later.

Just as Roxy arrived with Swanson's dinner and he began eating, Jim Talbot and Butch Grogan entered the saloon. Spying Swanson at his table, they walked over and greeted him.

"Bill, good to see you again," Talbot said. Swanson stood up and shook their hands. "Jim, Butch, good evening to you both. You are men of your word. You said you'd probably be here tonight. Please, have a seat. If you don't mind I'll keep at this, er, steak I ordered. Bit tough I'd say."

"Ah yes, Milly's Saturday night special," Talbot remarked as he and Grogan sat down. "That old cook back there, Sam I think is his name, still hasn't learned the fine art of preparing a steak dinner any more tender than the saddle on your horse. Beats me."

"Well, I've done some cooking in my time, including in the war. Maybe I can show him a few pointers."

"Every one of Milly's regulars would sure appreciate that," Talbot added, laughing. "Might turn Milly's into a right fine diner. Excuse me while I rustle up some beer. I'll be right back." Talbot rose and walked to the bar, where he found Milly hurriedly filling whiskey glasses.

"Why Sheriff, glad you're here. I see your friend from last week, Swanson, is back tonight. Roxy said she was pleased to see him. You looking for whiskey, beer, Marilee, all three? I think she's upstairs at the moment with Courtney. By the way, you seen Johnny lately? He was in here a while back, and he better get back here soon. You know about Courtney, don't you? She's carrying a little Indian in her belly, and Papa

Redfeather got some serious business in here to take care of. You see him, you tell him to get back here!"

"Milly, I will when I see him next. He knows, right?"

"Yeah, he knows, but he hasn't been in here to see Courtney in nearly two weeks. And as usual nobody knows where he's off to. I'll tell Marilee you are here. You want two whiskeys?"

"Make it three, one for the Colonel."

"Right, I'll get it over to you soon as I can."

"Thanks. No great rush."

Back at the table, Swanson was heavily engaged in a wrestling contest with his steak dinner. "Tough as a saddle doesn't exactly cut it. More like the wooden spoke of a wagon wheel," he complained as he leaned on his knife to saw off another chunk of meat. "Hardest damn chunk of beef I ever did eat. Or try to."

"Well, don't say I didn't warn you," Talbot chuckled. "Sooner you get to Sam about his cooking the better. Save all of us some teeth I'd bet. Doc Johnson always says he hates pulling teeth. Next time I see him I'll tell him you're planning to improve Sam's cooking. He'll appreciate that."

"Well, no promises. But might be a service I could extend to Milly. Say listen Jim, as I said last week I've been thinking I might like to do some hunting around here. I figure back up in these mountains there must be plenty of game, and I brought two good rifles with me from back east that I'd sure like to try using. Can you suggest some places I might go? I've heard talk of a few big canyons, Greens and also Reiser, and I'd appreciate the help of a guide. Be willing to pay him well, too. I might like to invest in some logging and building businesses too. Country out here sure is growing now that the damn war is over. Seems like a good time to invest, and I figure the more I know about the country out here the better. You know anyone I might hire as a guide?"

"Well, not sure but...." Just as Talbot began speaking, Jake Bulger, who had been sitting at a table a short distance away, pulled a chair up to their table and sat down. "Pardon my interruption, gentlemen, but I couldn't help hearing this gentleman asking about getting a hunting guide. My name's Jake Bulger, and I work for Jesse Smith running cattle back up in these canyons and valleys, so I know the land pretty well. I'm a hunter myself, and I'd sure be happy to take you out to some of the places where you might find some pretty good hunting, mostly elk, deer, some bighorn sheep maybe. Whatever you like I can probably lead you to it."

"Jesse Smith," Talbot interrupted immediately, "you work for Smith? That was Tompkin's operation a while back. How long you been with Smith? Were you working with Tompkin at all? I figure Mr. Swanson here needs to know that."

"Ah, er, no Sheriff, I was never with Tompkin. I only started working for Smith about the 17th of April or thereabouts. I came here from Texas. But yeah, I heard about Tompkin all right, what he and his men did up in Reiser Canyon. Heard it was a damn awful mess."

"Really! How do you know the attack was in Reiser?" Talbot asked immediately.

"Well, ah, some of the men back in the big bunkhouse still talk about it. Guess one or two who are left were at Reiser when the attack happened. That's all I know."

"I see," replied Talbot thoughtfully. "Just thought I should check, for Mr. Swanson's sake. So, where exactly you thinking of taking him hunting?"

"Oh, probably in the mountains east of here. Up in Greens Canyon, maybe Reiser. Or some of the smaller places out near Eagle Canyon. We sometimes take our herds near there for water, though I guess we're really not supposed to go there anymore. But sometimes we do, just for the water. It's huge, and really pretty. Got lots of deer, elk, maybe some big cats too."

"Well, as for Eagle Canyon," Talbot interjected, "Smith knows he's not supposed to run his herd there. That valley is sacred to Indians around here. Has been for centuries. Tompkin didn't give a damn about that, but I gather Smith has been more careful about not running his animals there. Anyway, I'd suggest you not hunt there."

"All right, guess that's reasonable, for now anyway. But lots of other places in these mountains to hunt."

"Say this sounds pretty good for now," Swanson responded. "Bulger, I do believe I will accept your offer. I'm staying up at the Dakota Hotel up around the corner. Let's plan on going out some time soon. You can leave me a message at the hotel, and I'll plan to meet you whenever you say. I'll work on getting provisions the next week or so. Just let me know when you're ready."

"I'll do that all right. Let's shake hands on that."

Swanson rose, and shook Bulger's hand. "Name's William Swanson. Care for a drink?"

"No thanks," Bulger said, "I need to ride back to the bunkhouse for the night. Mr. Swanson, I'll see you soon. Sheriff, Deputy, much obliged I'm sure." Bulger rose, tipped his hat, then walked toward the saloon's swinging doors. Sheriff Talbot looked at his deputy, sighed deeply, then turned to Swanson.

"Bill, listen to me. I have no way of knowing if Bulger is telling the truth about not being in Reiser Canyon and arriving later from Texas. But I would be careful being around any of Tompkin's herders. Just a bad lot. I guess there's really no reason for you to distrust Bulger, but the remaining herders, and maybe Bulger, may know that Johnny killed him at Reiser and saved my life. So, some of Tompkin's men might still want his scalp, and if that's true, you have to be really careful what you say about Johnny any time you're around Bulger. He's hurting enough, and as I told you last week his lady friend here, Darla, is pregnant. So he's suddenly got more to think about than he's used to. Just so you know, that's all."

"Jim, I sure appreciate knowing all that about Johnny. And I'll be careful, I promise you that. And I sure do hope I can find him out here soon. Say, how about another round here? I need another beer to wash down this horse leather I'm trying to finish."

"Fine idea," said Talbot. "I'll head over to the bar, be right back. Or at least I hope I'll be right back. Might talk with Marilee a bit. But won't be too long. Butch, check on some of those noisy card games over in gamblers' corner till I get back. And make sure somebody pays for the whiskey bottles that Roxy brings over."

"Sure thing, Sheriff."

10
Reunions

The evening sun lingered and danced on the west-facing walls of the White Mountains, painting their peaks myriad shades of vermillion and gold. By late May thousands of wildflowers in the meadows and river valleys, responding joyously to spring, perfumed the soothing light. Hawks and eagles floated high in the languid air. The inhabitants of Green River also welcomed the return of spring. Work on the approaching railroad had increased, and gangs of track layers, loggers, miners, and herders, as if suddenly risen from an icy cave, renewed their labors with increased vigor. Several of the town's shops, especially Jesse Wilkin's General Store and Erik Grady's "Welding, Supplies & Repairs," enjoyed increased business. The town's finer citizens, its "professional class" of business owners, bankers, a few lawyers, Doctor Mark Johnson, two nurses, an undertaker, and two new teachers, recently recruited from Denver to teach at the rebuilt school house, could frequently be seen riding the town's dusty streets in their buggies and be heard greeting their fellow citizens in a spirit of renewal heralded by the returning light and warmth.

About six o'clock on the evening of May 25th Johnny Redfeather strolled into Milly's saloon. The bar was already crowded, and the "dining room," where Milly kept tables and chairs for patrons desiring some of the saloon's dinner offerings, was already nearly full. Johnny walked right through the big room toward the bar, and was about to order a drink when Stella, one of the better shooting ladies from Johnny's army that had defended the saloon against Tompkin's attack, grabbed his leather vest and pulled him toward her.

"Well I'll be damned, if it isn't Johnny Redfeather. Sure nice to see you again. Where you been keeping yourself? I've not seen you in months."

"Why Miss Stella, sure is nice to see you again. Yeah, I've mostly been keeping to myself in a small cabin. Stowed away you might say, though I've been here a couple of times looking for Snuffy. Just didn't stay too long."

"Yeah, she's still really upset about losing Old Willie. They used to spend a lot of time together. She still sits out back trying to play his old guitar. Pretty damn sad, I must say, though he was about the only real friend Snuffy had in here. Rest of us can't stand her! Say, there's someone here needs to talk to you damn quick. Guess you know who I mean all right."

"Johnny Redfeather, get your damn red ass up here!" a voice boomed from the head of the stairs on the second floor. "Where the hell you been anyway?"

"Seems Courtney knows you're here," Stella laughed. "Better get on up there, I'd say."

"Yeah Stella, seems that way, doesn't it?" Johnny agreed. "Well, I'd better answer the call. See you around, Stella." He turned toward the stairs. "Sweet Darla dear, I'm coming right on up," Johnny shouted. "Just keep your britches in order till I get there." He ambled toward the far end of the saloon, then slowly mounted the stairs where Courtney Dillard, hands on hips and scowling, waited for him at the top.

"First, Mr. Redfeather, I told you last time my name is Courtney Dillard. And now it's Mama Courtney Dillard! I don't want any more of this damn Darla business. That part is over, was last New Year's Eve. Now follow me. We got to talk."

"Yes, Da... uh, Mama Courtney Dillard." She ushered Johnny into her room, and sat down on the bed. "Sit there," she ordered, pointing to a chair made of pine slabs and leather straps. "All right," she began, "now you got to sit and listen to me really good. Like I told you, I figured out this baby I'm carrying is yours, and I need to know what you're fixing to do about this little one. It is not going to grow up running around this crummy saloon like that Snuffy brat you call your 'lieutenant.' I won't have that. This kid gonna have a respectful life if I have to die to make that happen. Just cause I've been working in a saloon doesn't mean I don't have any dignity, don't deserve any respect. I'm sick of these damn railroad guys and them lousy, smelly herders from up valley and no-good saddle tramps that come through here thinking they can just take what they want from the women in here, slam their money on that table over in the corner, and just walk out and never bother with us afterwards. No more of that god-damn crap! You listening to me, daddy Redfeather?"

"Yes, Miss Mama Courtney Dillard. I sure am. I hear every little word you're saying!"

"Good, because I mean every damn little word I'm saying. I figure I'm near five months gone, so you don't have a lot of time to make arrangements for me and junior. He's, or she's, fixing to pop sometime in September I figure, and it's late May already. So, your turn now!"

"Mama Courtney Dillard," Johnny began, "I hear what you're saying all right. This is no place for a kid, especially an Indian kid. Snuffy never had a choice, and now that both her mama and papa are dead I figure whatever happens to her is up to me. You knew Old Willie was her father, right?"

"Yeah, I figured as much. Most people did. Way he always wanted to be around her. Showing her how to play that old guitar of his, pretending he knew how to play it himself. Cracked me up sometimes!"

"Yeah, well, I took her to Eagle Canyon, and told her about Old Willie being her father, and I said her mama was sure Indian, so like me she's part Indian. She's got to know about her Indian part, and the sooner that happens the better. She can't be here much longer. It would kill the Indian in her. I'm not about to let that happen, and the same goes for your little Indian in the oven. Right now I got a cabin up in Raven Mountain, mostly where I stay now. Not much, but it's something anyway. No reason to go back to Reiser Canyon, nothing left there. Nothing! So I figure on making this cabin a little place for us for a while. I can make it so it's warmer for winter. Got time to do that now. I hunt, fish, we could maybe grow some food. Maybe later think about something closer to town. Maybe find some work here, with the Sheriff maybe. He owes me a couple times over, so I figure maybe he'd hire me on. But the Indian part I'm never letting go, not for me, not for Snuffy, not for junior growing under your big skirt."

Courtney Dillard lay back on her bed and sighed deeply. "So, we're gonna raise this kid up in some deserted canyon somewhere far out of town, just so he can be a brave little Indian. That right? And with Snuffy I take it? That's your idea, Papa Indian?"

"Now you listen to me, Mama Courtney! You got to give me time to work all this out. Don't rush me! No need for that now, not yet. You just take care of that little Indian in your belly, and I'll do what's necessary for the rest. Trust me."

"Yeah, well last time you said that to me, here comes this little surprise. Milly hasn't said much since I told her about this, but now that I'm pregnant I'm not fixing to work late nights around here anymore, if you follow me. I can still serve all those no-good bums in here food and whiskey all right, but nothing more."

"I sure do understand that, Mama Darla. And that's damn good. Now you take care. I'll be around here more often now. Got to find the sheriff, maybe talk to him. Seeing as how it's a Saturday, he might be here later. I'll wander down there, see if he's here yet. You coming down?"

"Yeah, I'm coming down. I told Milly I'd be glad to work behind the bar tonight. Milly said that way Frank can keep all them herders and railroad bums away from me. Said tonight he'd have two pistols behind the bar, just in case some fool doesn't understand the word "No," or is too stupid to realize that my oven is baking, as you might say. Tell Milly I'll be right there. And stop calling me Darla! I'm not just Darla. I'm Mama Courtney Dillard!"

"Yes, Miss Mama Courtney Dillard!" Redfeather stood up and leaned over Courtney lying on the bed. He gently kissed her lips, then caressed her belly. "Little Indian, whatever your name is, you keep on growing in there. Papa Redfeather will make a fine life for you one of these days. You just wait, and don't cause your Mama here too much trouble. Ya hear?" He winked at Courtney, then slipped into the hall and sauntered down the stairs and into the noisy throng enjoying another exuberant Saturday night in Milly's Green River Saloon.

§

Later that evening Colonel Swanson strode into Milly's from the Dakota Hotel. He spotted Sheriff Talbot seated at a table near the bar talking to Marilee and walked over to join them.

"Jim, Miss Marilee—did I get that right? —mind if I join you?" he asked politely. "I hope I'm not interfering. Just hoped I'd see Jim here for a few moments. Mind if I sit down?"

"Why no, Colonel. We were just chatting. Nothing too serious. Not yet anyway. That right, Jim?" Marilee asked.

"I'd say that's about right, Marilee," Talbot responded. "Perhaps we can talk again later. Bill, have a seat."

"I'll leave you two gentlemen to whatever it is the Colonel here has to ask you about. You just let me know if you need anything later. I'll be here."

"I believe I'll have a whiskey," Swanson said. "And one here for my friend Jim."

"Sure thing. Coming right up. Won't take but a few minutes. Pretty busy all of a sudden."

"Now Marilee don't you fret on our account. We aren't going anywhere else tonight. Whenever is fine," Talbot assured her.

Marilee glanced at Talbot. "Always the gentleman! Guess Abigail had good reason to call you that," she added as she headed back toward the bar.

"Abigail? That your wife? My apologies, Jim. I didn't realize you are married," Swanson said.

"Was married. My wife, Abigail, was killed here in town last July. Crazy man coming out of Hal's Saloon, firing every which way. Stray bullet pierced her skull. Nothing Doc Johnson could do." Talbot looked down and sighed.

"Jim, so sorry. If you want me to come back later...."

Talbot looked up. "Oh no, no, that's all in the past now. I'm sure Marilee meant no harm. Abigail used to call me 'Gentleman Jim' back in Virginia, that's all. So, Bill, as I think you said the other night you prefer, what's on your mind that maybe I can help you with?"

"Well, Jim as you know this fellow Jake, Bulger I think his last name is, offered to take me hunting here last week. Now, seeing as how I'm new here, and I know you've been here much longer, I wondered if you could tell me anything more about him. I know nothing about him beyond what you told me last Saturday night. Now when we talked here last week Bulger said he came from Texas, and wasn't with the raid at Reiser Canyon on that Indian tribe. Well, as you said then, maybe he's telling the truth about that, and maybe he isn't. But hell, thousands who survived that god-damn war are coming west, and if he was a Rebel, and he sure sounds like he was, then I sure would like to know if he was anywhere near Georgia late in sixty-four. Just in case he knows more than I'd like him to."

"Well, Bill, I have been back to Tompkin's, or Smith's, place since that attack on Running Bear's tribe, and I didn't know too many of his original herders. A couple I knew are dead, including one real mean bastard named Curly. Anyway, I can try to find out more about Bulger, maybe write marshals back east. But I'd be careful about what you say to him. He doesn't have to know too much about you, and if you don't ask too much about him, maybe he'll not pester you too much either. Either way, maybe the less you know about each other right now the better. That make sense to you?"

"Yes, sure. He left me a note at the hotel, saying maybe we'd go out this next week. I just thought I'd try to find out what more you might know about him. He seems like a nice fellow all right, but a lot of men I met in the war were more devil than human."

"Don't I know that! Lord almighty, don't I know that!" Talbot exclaimed.

"I'll be all go to hell! You some kind of god-damn ghost? What grave did you come out of?" Johnny Redfeather thundered suddenly from the bar as heads turned in his direction. "Colonel William Swanson, is that really you?"

"Johnny," Swanson yelled as he stood up. "I heard you were here! God-damnit! I can't believe I'm actually seeing you again!"

"Well, you're the one supposed to be dead! Not me!" Redfeather yelled, as he and Swanson raced toward each other in the middle of the saloon. As they embraced, yelping and vigorously slapping each other's back, cheers and cries of "Ain't that something," "Wonderful," and "I'll be damned" suddenly boomed all around the saloon. Couples at tables stood and cheered. Milly clapped loudly, then yelled "God isn't this just terrific?" then ordered Roxy and Marilee to prepare a round of whiskey for Redfeather and Swanson, and Sheriff Talbot too. "This here calls for a little celebration!" Milly proclaimed to more cheers. "Not every day we see something like this in a saloon! You all sit down at a bigger table over closer to the bar and I'll have Marilee and Roxy bring you some of our finer whiskey. Marilee, Roxy, fetch a new bottle and three glasses. On the house, you agree Frank?"

"For sure, Milly," Frank agreed from behind the bar. "Hey Charley," Frank yelled, "how about something for a reunion party. Can you do that?"

"Yeah I think so," Charley yelled back, and proceeded to pound even harder on randomly selected keys of his dilapidated piano, assuming that an increase in volume would make whatever tune he thought he might be playing automatically more festive.

Amid more exalted shouting and clapping, Milly led Swanson, Redfeather and Talbot to their table, followed by Roxy and Marilee with a tray full of whiskey glasses and a fresh bottle. "Now you all just have a grand ole time here, seeing as how it's like you both come back from the dead," Milly shouted gleefully. "What a hell of a surprise! On the house!"

The men sat down and Marilee opened the bottle and poured generous amounts of whiskey into all three glasses. "Now you three just party away!" she exclaimed. "And when you finish this bottle, just let me know and I'll fetch another one."

"Thank you kindly," Talbot replied. The men raised, clinked, then swiftly emptied their glasses. Swanson quickly refilled them as Redfeather nodded to Talbot, who returned the gesture, then glared straight at Swanson, as if seeing a ghost. "Colonel, drunk or sober I can't believe these Indian eyes! Sheriff here told me last summer you'd been murdered. Isn't that right Sheriff?"

"That's right, Johnny," Talbot said. "That's what I'd been told by a man in the General Store who said he knew Colonel Swanson in the war. Said he'd heard he'd been killed in Colorado in spring of sixty-six by a rebel who'd recognized him from someplace down South. Georgia, I think he said."

"Yeah, god-damn, it would have to be Georgia all right," Swanson replied. The men downed their second shot, and Talbot, assuming Swanson was about to tell his story, refilled them again.

"Well, damn near was. Twice. Some damn fool down in Georgia near the end didn't know there was a cease-fire and kept firing. Lousy shot. Got himself killed a few seconds later, but a bullet just skimmed my left temple and knocked me down flat. Maybe some Rebel thought I was dead. Got a big old scar under this Stetson. Second time in Kansas Territory about a year ago. I was staying in St. Charles, thinking about maybe making some investments in gold mining. Crazy panners all over the landscape. Well, one guy accused me of cheating him, pulled a gun. Clumsy damn fool, way too slow. I killed him easily. Marshal said self-defense, so that was that. I'm not sure which report of my death you heard, Jim. But as you see, both were wrong."

"Yeah they sure are! What the hell you doing here?" Redfeather asked.

"Well, since the railroad's heading west fast, I decided I'd come see more of the new Dakota Territory. Maybe look to some investing out here. I got no family, so after the war, and then my father's death, I figured I'd strike out, join the crowds coming out here. Thought I'd try to find a place where no one talked about war anymore."

"I sure appreciate that," Talbot added. "Seems every man I meet out here wants to forget that damn war. Can't say as how I blame them."

"Johnny," Swanson began, "what's your story? You had to avoid both Rebels and Yanks after we split up. And those damn snakes! How'd you manage these last years?"

"Well, like I told Sheriff Talbot many times, Indians know how to survive. I lived with tribes all the way up from Georgia and Tennessee, traveled when I could. Stole a few horses when I had to. Doesn't bother me now. I knew some of the Cheyenne were still up in these parts, so wanted to get here before they were all gone. Aren't many Indians left it seems. Sheriff here can tell you about what happened to Running Bear's tribe up in Reiser Canyon a while back. I can't stay there anymore, and seems now I got some reasons to stay more in town. But I got a cabin up in the mountains where I stay if I'm not here or out hunting. Maybe you come see it one day. Good hunting up in those valleys."

"Hell yes, I'd like that Johnny! You and me could sure use some time together. This fellow Bulger I met in here a week or so ago also invited me to go hunting with him, but he can wait. Jim says Bulger is working for this man Smith, who I gather took over for this Tompkin guy who attacked the Indians up in Reiser Canyon. Is that about right, Jim?"

"Yes, that's right. Mean son-of-a-bitch he was! Johnny knows all about him. He slit Tompkin's throat just as he was about to shoot me that day!"

"That right? Johnny! Still slitting throats and saving white men's asses, are you? You sure are good at that. Saved mine back at that prisoner camp in Georgia for sure!"

"Yeah, seems I got some sort of knack of knowing when to show up. Maybe someday some white man could return the favor. That'd sure be welcome."

"Johnny, you got my word on that," Swanson said. "No question about that if the occasion arises. You agree, Jim, after what you just said?"

"Absolutely," Talbot added. "Let's toast to that, shall we? Bottoms up!"

The three men clinked glasses and finished their whiskey. "Gentlemen, I got to get upstairs now to attend to my Darla, er, Mama Courtney Dillard. So you will excuse me," Redfeather said. He rose, extended his right hand to Swanson, and when Swanson stood and offered his right hand, Johnny gripped his forearm tightly. In return Swanson gripped Redfeather's forearm. "Ha," Redfeather said, "you remember! Like I said once to the Sheriff here in this saloon, we have fought together in the cause of justice, even if it wasn't perfect. So Colonel, like I said back in Georgia, I consider us brothers. You, like me, have survived, and I sure am glad you have come back from wherever you've been, which I guess wasn't a grave after all."

"Johnny, you have returned from war and survived those damn snakes and Lord knows what else. Damn near a miracle I'd say, seeing you again. I'm staying at the Dakota Hotel, Room 14. You come by or leave a message for me when you can, and we'll go hunting for sure. If this Bulger guy shows up, I'll tell him hunting with him will just have to wait. I got to spend more time with Johnny Redfeather."

"How you men doing with your whiskey there?" Marilee asked as she approached their table.

"We're doing just fine," Swanson asserted. "Just fine. I gather Johnny here has some business to see about, but I believe Jim and I can do some more damage to this bottle for the rest of the evening. Agreed, Jim?"

"Agreed." Talbot stood and turned to face Redfeather. "Johnny, guess now I'll see you around town. Best you get on up to Miss Dillard now."

"Guess so, Sheriff. Right good to see you again."

"Likewise, Johnny, I'm sure." As Redfeather turned to leave, Talbot tapped him on the shoulder, and Redfeather nodded as he walked away. Standing at the corner of the bar, as if waiting for him, was Snuffy. "Lieutenant," Redfeather barked, "git on up to Darla's with me. We got some talking to do."

"You got more Indian stuff to tell me I reckon," Snuffy quipped. "I can tell by the look on your face."

"Never mind the look on my face. Just get up there," Redfeather said as he headed toward the stairs at the far end of the bar.

Talbot turned to Marilee. "Marilee, thanks for checking on us. Ask

Sam to cook us a couple steaks, will you? On the tender side, if that's possible. I got to walk around, see how Butch is doing with the card games and all the other kinds of trouble people can get into here. I'll find you later tonight. Bill, you'll excuse me for a few minutes. I won't be long."

"Sure thing, Jim. Say Marilee, is Roxy here tonight? I might like to talk to her again."

"Yeah, she's here. I'll tell her you were asking about her. Send her over to your table. So Jim maybe I'll see you later tonight then?"

"Yes, I'll make a point of that, Marilee. William, don't go anywhere. Be back quick as I can."

"That sounds just fine, Jim. Much obliged."

"Sure thing," Talbot said as he waded into the assortment of characters pursuing the myriad pleasures available for the asking on a late spring evening at the Green River Saloon.

11
Sunday Morning

"I'm not always nasty to him, am I? Is that what it seems to everyone at the saloon? Did Milly say that?" Courtney asked Marilee as they sat together on an old bench in a small wooded area near the Presbyterian church.

"Yes, Milly said that. Even Frank, who pretty much minds his own business, agreed with Milly. And Roxy and Stella hear you getting on him whenever you two are together in your room. Roxy said she wonders why he even spends any time with you. Man gets no peace at all, she told me."

"Well, lately he's hardly here, says he's off in a cabin somewhere in the mountains, and we got some serious talking to do about the future, which for most of my life I never thought would be important. Fact is most of my life I never even thought I would have a future. Just one lousy night after another in that crummy saloon. Not much else for a woman to do in a dusty town like this. I wasn't planning' on having this kid, and I got to be damn sure I don't end up raising it all by myself."

"Courtney, I understand all that, but you can't deny that you've been fascinated by Redfeather for a long time. We both know that last New Year's Eve wasn't a sudden fluke. And Johnny may not always be around, but at least you know he's your kid's father, and that puts you ahead of a lot of women in our situation. Johnny just might be your ticket out of Milly's, which I don't mind saying I envy. Seems to me you might want to think about that possibility. You just might have more of a future than you think."

"Well, he's cute, and yes I do find him attractive. Guess that's obvious now. I never knew what most folks call a family, just bounced around from one filthy mining or logging camp to another. Never knew who my father was, and don't remember much about my mother either, drunk or sober. Maybe I'm just so scared and angry all the time to believe what any man says to me. I don't know know how to be nice because no one was ever nice to me. Yeah, Johnny is good and warm when he is around, and I'm just so damn scared he'll leave one day and never come back. Then it'd be me and this kid all alone in a saloon with those stinking drunks pawing at me all night."

"Aren't you speaking truth there, Courtney?"

"Maybe I just don't know any other way to keep what I want besides scratching and clawing, like a big cat protecting a kill. 'This is mine, goddamnit! Get away!' Or like trying to get food in a mining camp when your mother is off with her bottle and a different man every night. Mean and nasty, that's about all I know. Sad, isn't it?"

"Courtney, far from me to judge. I'm just saying that maybe Johnny Redfeather might prove to be more decent and caring than you give him credit for. Lord knows how many chances I'd give Sheriff Talbot if he'd come out of his shell and just try to build a life with me. Don't I know that. That man is all locked up inside. Johnny Redfeather, whatever else you say about him, is not locked up."

"Yes, that's for sure," Courtney laughed as she patted her tummy. "Not locked up at all."

"We best get back," Marilee said, "Milly and Frank will be opening soon. We got to earn our keep, like it or not. Think about what I said. The women and I want you and Johnny and the little one to try to be happy together, one way or another. Not easy out here in this awful wilderness, but maybe not impossible either. You just have to work harder at whatever it is you want."

Courtney looked at Marilee, then reached out and embraced her. "Nice to hear that somebody else really cares. I'm not used to that. Thanks."

"Sure thing, Courtney. Let's go."

12
Johnny Redfeather's Cabin

"Can I help you?" the clerk asked Redfeather at the Dakota Hotel several days later.

"Yeah, is Colonel William Swanson here?"

"No, he left around nine o'clock this morning. Said he had to see a man about a horse and then the General Store about some gear. Something about hunting I figure."

"Ah, right. We're planning on going together someday soon. Well, if you could just give him this note when he returns. I'd be much obliged."

"Yeah, I can do that all right. Who should I say left it?"

"Johnny Redfeather. He's expecting it."

"Okay. I'll put it in his mailbox, see to it that he gets it soon as he returns."

"That's right kind," Redfeather replied and walked back onto the street where Courtney Dillard and Amanda waited for him. "All right you two, time to get on these horses and head out. We got us a long ride today."

"Where exactly you figurin' on takin' us, Papa Redfeather, if you don't mind me asking?" Courtney asked.

"Your new mountain home Darla, er, Mama Courtney. Nice little cabin I fixed up in a clearing up on Raven Mountain. Got everything you could possibly hope for. You have to get used to this place, you and Amanda. Isn't that right, Lieutenant?"

"I reckon, if you say so. Johnny, are we gonna sleep up there in this cabin? Stay there a while? Aren't I coming back to Milly's ever?"

"You all will be going back. You and Mama here. This is just for a time. Indian time, you might say. We all got some figuring out to do, the three of us, or four I guess it is now, and we got to talk some more about what I told you up at Eagle Canyon a while back. We aren't finished talking about all that, not by a long shot. Now Mama get on over here so's I can get you up on this horse. You ride in front of me, and hold onto these saddle bags while we ride. Don't want to lose any of this grub. Now come on, give me your left foot, and then you'll swing on over."

"Johnny Redfeather, you damn rattlesnake, I've never been on a horse in my life for longer than ten minutes. How do I know this isn't some plot to abandon both of us? I knew I never should have trusted you! Where we riding to anyway?"

"Up to the mountain, I told you."

"For how long?"

"Well depends on how fast we ride I suppose. If we just keep riding slow, maybe five, six, seven hours, figuring with two and then some on this horse, plus this food we're carrying. It won't be really fast. Don't want to torture my horse you know. He's a good riding horse, been really good to me. So I got to treat him nice. Plus part of this trail is quite steep up close to the summit, so we have to be considerate toward our transportation."

"Seems you more interested in how you treat this horse than how you treat me and this little bundle in my belly. How did I ever get mixed up with you back in that damn saloon anyway?"

"Well, must have been my Indian charm!"

"Charm? Who said anything about charm?"

"I did. Now let's go!"

"Well, god-damnit, help me up here!"

Johnny lifted Courtney up onto the saddle in one swift movement. "There you be, nice and comfortable. Now hush up that cursing in front of this child here, and let's get going. "

"Who you calling' a child, Johnny?" Amanda quipped. "I'm no child. Milly tells me I'm nearly thirteen now."

"Thirteen! Now isn't that just something? Thirteen! Amanda, you ride this other good horse and carry more of the saddlebags. I got its bridle tied by a rope to my saddle so's it'll just follow me and Mama. Don't worry, you'll be fine. Up you go!" Johnny lifted Amanda onto her horse, then swung onto the back of his horse and pointed the animal toward Raven Mountain. "Alright, Nomonehe'se, here we go!"

Nearly two hours later, after a slow ride punctuated by Courtney Dillard's frequent complaints about how uncomfortable she was, Johnny

Redfeather guided his horse out of the forest and into Raven Meadow. Wildflowers of a hundred hues carpeted the meadow, basking in the warmth of the early summer sun. Enchanted by a gentle breeze the flowers danced to a melody only they could hear, a bending, curving, swaying kaleidoscope of red and blue and yellow and green that Johnny Redfeather thought must be left over from the paradise he had once heard about from a preacher in Florida. "This paradise was made just for Indians," he thought. "Maybe bring Running Bear back up here. Might do him some good. Never know."

Suddenly Johnny's horse whinnied loudly and jumped back, alarmed by its sense of another creature nearby. Redfeather looked to his left and saw fifty yards away the grizzly sow and her cubs that he had seen when descending the mountain several days ago. The bear stood upright, on alert for her cubs. As the horse stumbled back, Courtney Dillard screamed and behind him Amanda yelled, "Johnny, now what?" as her horse strained against the rope tied to its bridle.

"Johnny, god-damnit," Courtney cried, "you are trying to kill us all! What do we do now? Won't that bear attack?"

"Hush, both of you! Mama grizzly isn't interested in us. Just be quiet. I got a rifle here just in case we need it, but we won't. She's teaching her cubs to find food, berries and stuff, and we aren't food for a grizzly. Long as we don't get any closer, she won't pay us any mind. Told you these were good horses, they knew the bear was there before we did. Isn't that right, Amanda?"

"If you say so, Johnny. But that bear is huge!"

"Huge means nothing as long as we behave. You got to learn about bears, the big cats, everything else that's out here, Amanda. Even rattlesnakes down here in this meadow. Also spirits you can't rightly see but that are here anyway, just because they want to be. Told you before, up at Eagle Canyon, it's time you learn about Indian ways out here, cause like me you're part Indian and you got to know what that means. Same as Mama Dillard's little one comin' on. That's what this ride is all about. Now we got to get by mama grizzly. Come on, horse, easy now. Real slow. Mama Dillard, just be quiet and stop shaking."

"How I'm supposed to stop shaking? I'm scared half-dead. You damn Indian, you're nothing but trouble."

"Shhh, Courtney. Don't scare mama grizzly now. Grizzlies have excellent hearing. Be quiet while I get us further up this trail. Can't just sit here all day. He'kotoo'estse, sit still and calm down. Hush now, Mama. Hush." Johnny looked behind him. "Amanda, let's go. Your horse will be fine. He'll follow us up the trail."

Redfeather gently urged his horse forward, alternately looking at the trail ahead and then at the bear. The sow remained standing, staring, for another minute, her cubs gathered around her huge back paws, before lowering itself. Redfeather stroked his horse's left flank, trying to calm it and keep it from whinnying or, worse, bolting suddenly. The horse nodded several times, as if responding to Redfeather's calming touch, then began plodding forward, picking its way carefully among the stones and tree roots on the trail. In front of them Raven Mountain loomed, its mammoth, rocky arms seemingly stretched out wide to embrace them as they slowly approached. At the eastern edge of the meadow, as the foothills begin sweeping gradually upward, Redfeather spotted the beginning of the narrow trail that leads up to the summit of Raven Mountain and eventually to his cabin.

§

Several hours later, after guiding his horse and Amanda's behind him over the slippery rocks approaching the summit, Redfeather gingerly led the animals over the mountain's last craggy ridge. Just past the summit the forested valley far down the mountain's eastern slope gradually opened before them.

"Where the hell we going now Redfeather, if you don't mind me asking?" Courtney bellowed as she gazed into the distance. "We're not going down into that valley, are we? There's nothing there!"

"Hell there isn't! There's a nice little cabin down there that's just right for us. Old hunting cabin I found and fixed up. Now hang on so's this horse can get us down there all in one piece, if you get my meaning. The rest of this trail is rocky and narrow, and we can't rattle these horses any more than they already are. Now hush and hang on. You too back there, Lieutenant Amanda."

"I'm hanging," Amanda cried, "but you and your horse better know where we're heading, cause like Courtney said I don't see anything to ride to."

"You will. You will."

They descended slowly into the unfolding forest. Stands of oaks, cottonwoods, juniper berry, white pines and occasional Douglas firs wove shades of green into random patterns set boldly against the snowy peaks beyond. Clusters of mountain wildflowers—fireweed, paintbrush, columbine, bluebell, larkspur, red clover— unfurled on either side of the trail in waves of vibrant colors that cascaded toward the valley below. Paradise, Johnny reflected again; Indian paradise!

As they rode around a bend, Johnny's small, ramshackle cabin suddenly appeared.

"There it is! Just like I left it. Told you it was there!"

"Well who the hell would put a cabin way up here?" shouted Courtney. "Middle of damn nowhere, I swear."

"Indians, that's who! Nice little place for Indians hunting in these mountains where there's no white people to bother them. Just right for us. Now hang on, we got some steep trail ahead. Won't take long now," Redfeather assured his passengers.

When they finally reached the cabin Redfeather dismounted, then helped Courtney and Amanda down off their horses before tying both animals to a tree. "All right ladies, you wait here while I check for critters in the cabin. Don't want to surprise any visitors. Real bad idea!"

"Critters? Now you want us to sleep in a cabin with animals? You're trying to kill us, aren't you?" shouted Courtney. "Amanda, tell this fool we're not going in there! What makes you think people can live here? There any snakes up here? Amanda...."

"Mama Courtney, just hush up a minute! Maybe Johnny knows what to do. Maybe 'cause he's Indian he knows how to live up here. Isn't that what you told me up at Eagle Canyon a while back, Johnny? Learning Indian ways?"

"Yeah, something like that I believe. Not that hard, really. Now you two just wait here a minute, and I'll be right back. And Mama, there aren't any snakes here. Too damn high and cold for them."

"You damn well better be right about that!" Courtney exclaimed. "I'm not planning' on dying all alone up here."

"You won't die up here," Redfeather replied, and headed for the cabin. He pushed open the large door, noticed his hatchet still hanging on the far wall, and carefully walked inside. Seeing nothing, he walked outside only to spot a large coyote lurking near the corner of the cabin. "Coyote, git!" he yelled and shot at its feet as the animal sprinted away. Courtney screamed and pulled Amanda in front of her.

"Hush now, it's gone," Redfeather proclaimed. "No bother now."

"Well, what if it's got little coyotes, like that damn bear back there? Then what?" demanded Courtney, backing up and pulling Amanda tighter around her.

"Then I'll scare them away too. Now get on in here before it starts getting dark. We need to store this grub, light a lantern, make a fire, and get our bedrolls set up. Now stop shaking, let go of that child there, and help unload our horses so I can feed them and put blankets on them for the night."

Two hours later, having stowed their clothes and food and finished a supper of beans and salted meat that Johnny had cooked, they sat, huddled in heavy blankets, on wooden benches near the small fire place. As evening descended, and with it a sense of calm after their long and perilous ride, Johnny Redfeather recalled similar evenings when the sheer vastness of this wilderness, its serene stillness, and billions upon billions of shimmering lights above comforted him with that most elusive of all emotions: hope. Initially in Reiser Canyon with Running Bear, and especially alone in Eagle Canyon, Redfeather hoped that somehow the mountains themselves could preserve that part of him that he identified as Indian. And, on this secluded plateau below the eastern rim of Raven Mountain, he desperately hoped that Amanda and Courtney could begin to sense what just being on this mountain could teach them about their present and perhaps their future lives.

"Now, Otahe! Listen up, both of you," Johnny began. "This little talk is about all of us. Me, Mama's and my little one, and you Amanda are all part Indian, and that's the most important part. Most white people, who know nothing important about Indian people, like to call us half-breed, like me because my daddy was Irish and my mama was Indian, way back Cheyenne she liked to say. If so, then Tsis-tsitas is my right Indian name. So, on my mama's side your little one, Mama Courtney, is Tsis-tsitas too. Half-breed is never a good term for Indian people, not even mixed like us. Indian is Indian, don't matter what part or parts. Amanda, your daddy was Old Willie all right, and he probably figured that out right quick once he got to Milly's and saw you, but your mama was Indian. Like I told you at Eagle Canyon, maybe Apache, Comanche, Navajo, not quite sure, but surely from south of here. Willie called her "Mexican," but she was Indian all right, so that's what you are, Indian, and from your mother, Amanda. Just like me."

"So you gonna be my daddy now? Make me an Indian girl that takes snuff? What about Milly and her women? They're not all bad just because they're white," Amanda complained. "Aren't I ever going back there? I got to stay up here with these creepy snakes and other critters?"

"No, you're going back there. But that life for you at Milly's in town is no good for you, or at least for your Indian part. You got to learn Indian ways, about these mountains, their animals, stories, spirits, whatever language I can teach you—not much, but some—and how to live like an Indian, especially out here, under these stars. I know there isn't really much Indian land left, except maybe Eagle Canyon where I took you a while back. The whites and their damn railroad, what Running Bear called the 'fire wagon,' are fixing to claim it all and drive us away. But I'll be all go to hell I can hardly figure where to anymore. But that doesn't mean they can drive away what all is Indian inside you. You've got to believe that. And I know Milly and those women at her saloon all say they're trying to raise you, but you spend all your time there and pretty soon it'll be too late for you to recognize any of that Indian part. So, from now on you're going to spend some time with me and Mama Courtney here in this little cabin, up in these mountains, down in Eagle Canyon too. Best I can do at the moment. You just can't go too much longer in your life without understanding where you really came from. You see that?"

"Yeah, I guess I do. I guess I got to now. Don't have too much choice I see."

"So, Daddy Redfeather," Courtney interrupted, "what about me? And this kid I'm carrying? We gonna be out here too, bears and snakes and God knows what else? This is no place to raise a child!"

"And you think a god-damn saloon is? "

"Well, least Milly got big pot stoves and warm beds, and there's no snakes in that saloon."

"Yeah, but there are many different kinds of snakes. Cowboys, panners, railroad workers coming after Indians and shooting women and children! That's a worse kind of snake any day! I'll make this place warm enough any time you're here, don't worry. That blanket you got yourself all wrapped up in could keep two mama bears warm any damn night. Don't you worry about that. You can get back to Milly's stoves and beds all right, but for now, when it's warmer, we'll spend some time in this cabin, in these mountains with the spirits, like Maheo, Wihio, maybe even Nonoma, thunder spirit. Maybe Hestovatohkeo'o, Two-Face. Nobody ever knows where it is or even if it's even in these mountains. You got to learn about them too."

"Who? What?" snapped Courtney. "You just making me more convinced you really are a no-good lunatic! Even that mean ole preacher in town doesn't use words like that!"

"That's because that preacher doesn't know any Cheyenne words. But I do, 'cause that's what my mama taught me. And you got to learn some Cheyenne words too, since we're a part-Indian family now. Won't be that hard. You'll see. But no use worrying about that now. It's getting dark. Let's arrange these bedrolls and these cots I made. Time to sleep. Mama, you and me over here. Amanda, you're over there beneath that window I fixed. No snake or bear getting' in here anymore! We'll talk more tomorrow."

Johnny watched Courtney sliding beneath the wool blankets she had spread over their cot. After he lay down he reached under her blanket and gently stroked her womb, then kissed her cheek. "Ne'esehosotomoo'estse," he said. "You rest now."

"That's real sweet, Johnny. I don't know that big long word, but resting feels really good right now. So does your hand on my tummy. You sure can be nice when you want to be."

"Course I can," Johnny replied.

"Guess I could try to be nice too, couldn't I? Johnny, do you really want to be with me? Do you want to be a father?"

"Yes and yes. Now rest, Mama Courtney Dillard."

§

At sunrise Johnny Redfeather stood facing east on the plateau in front of the cabin. He wore buffalo-hide moccasins, heavy denim pants, a buckskin vest, and a denim shirt. Around his neck dangled a silver chain to which was attached a turquoise medallion in the shape of a bear paw. He had received the medallion from a Navajo medicine man during his long journey north and west after his escape from the prisoner camp in Georgia. In his hand he held four arrows, wrapped in buffalo hide and scented with sage. Each arrow was decorated with eagle feathers: two with shafts painted black, two with shafts painted red. He walked to the center of a large circle he had laid out with rocks in front of his cabin. In the middle of this circle was a smaller ring of stones. He lifted the arrows toward the sun, then crossed them over his chest and held them there for several seconds. He then knelt, bowed his head, and prayed to Maheo, the Creator, repeating the words that his mother had taught him when they lived in Florida, very far away from their tribal roots on the plains and the northern mountains.

Johnny then rose, walked out to the larger circle, and walking around it placed one of the arrows at each of the four directions: the red painted arrows pointed north and south, and the black painted arrows pointed west and east. He then returned to the center of the smaller ring, knelt again for several seconds, then stood, walked back to the perimeter of the larger circle, and began to move, slowly at first then gradually more quickly, around the circle, gently swaying his body to an imagined rhythm of chanting and drumming. As he moved he pointed toward the sun and then toward the four directions, seeking to find the spiritual guidance that his mother had told him once blessed and protected the Cheyenne People and that he desperately hoped to invoke with his ritual movements. For nearly an hour he swayed and danced, jumping slightly first on one foot and then the other, his mother's enchanting words echoing in his memory, reminding him of what deep within himself he feared to lose. "Hi-niswa' vita' ki' ni. Hi-niswa' vita' ki' ni," he chanted as he danced. The spring sun cast his shadow, creating an illusionary second Cheyenne brave, before, behind, and beside him on his clockwise path around the circle. "Maheo, bless me, bless my shadow, bless our tribe. Hi-niswa' vita' ki' ni."

"Johnny, why are you walking around in circles? Have you lost your mind for good?" Courtney barked at him from the door of the cabin. "I got a little Indian in my belly and his father is walking around in circles like he's got no damn idea where he's headed!"

Johnny stopped, and looked over his shoulder at Courtney and Amanda, who stood just behind Courtney. "Mama, hush! Leave me alone for now. Can't you see I'm dancing? This is important. Now hush!"

"Since when is goin' around in a circle important? That won't get you anywhere that I can see. Isn't that right, Amanda?"

"Courtney, Johnny Redfeather usually knows what he's talking about, except maybe on New Year's Eve when he's lying about how many men he's killed. So I wouldn't be so sure he doesn't know what he's doing now. Maybe we just have to let him explain."

"You tell her, lieutenant!" Johnny yelled. "Now Darla, you and Amanda go fix up some of them eggs and bacon I brought, and leave me be for a while longer. I'm not done dancing for this morning. While we're eating I'll explain about the arrows. It's important!"

"How many damn times I told you not to call me Darla? Haven't you learned that yet? Seems I got to remind you about that twice every day, and that's still not enough for you to remember. Come on, Amanda, let's leave this man walking in a circle to nowhere. I'm hungry. You get the fire going and I'll find the grub."

"Yes, Darla."

"Courtney! Mama Courtney Dillard! You're as hard at learning anything as he is!"

"Yes, Mama Courtney Dillard, I reckon you're right about that."

For several more minutes Redfeather continued his chanting and rhythmic movements around the stone circle, accompanied only by his shadow and a fragile hope in what he dimly remembered about the Cheyenne ceremonies and rituals. "O Maheo, Creator, make me whole. Make me whole," he prayed as he moved. When he sensed it was time to stop, he gathered the four arrows, wrapped them again in the buffalo hide containing the sage leaves, and walked into the cabin. "Time to talk," he thought. "Amanda got to know more about who she is, what she has to do. Where she needs to be even. Poor little Indian growing inside a white woman. What have I done?" he wondered. "What have I done?"

§

"Now that was a damn fine breakfast, I must say," Redfeather remarked after they had finished eating as they sat before the small fireplace. "You'll be a real good cook for our little Cheyenne, Mama Courtney."

"Never you mind my cooking, Johnny. My little Cheyenne, as you call it, deserves to know why its nutty father walks in circles so early in the morning, getting nowhere."

"It's not nutty, Mama. It's something you have to understand. Those four arrows are Maahotse, Sacred Arrows the Cheyenne call them. Or in some stories, Ma-huts, the Medicine Arrows. There are several stories about these arrows, and also about the dances, going far back in Cheyenne time. The stories about the Sun Dance, or the Medicine

Dance or Ghost Dance in some versions, talk of how a brave named Sweet Medicine journeyed to a far-off mountain reaching high into the sky, and when he rolled back a huge rock at the base of the mountain and entered he found himself in a great medicine lodge. There Maheo the Creator and his helper, Great Roaring Thunder, instructed him for a long time about what he must teach his people. When Sweet Medicine was about to leave, Maheo showed him four arrows decorated with hawk feathers and four with eagle feathers, and told him to choose. Sweet Medicine chose the arrows decorated with eagle feathers, and Maheo said he had chosen rightly and that those arrows would protect his people because the eagle was the strongest and bravest bird. Two of the arrows' shafts were painted black, and two were painted red. And the stories say that before Sweet Medicine left the mountain Maheo taught him how to make arrows like the eagle arrows Maheo had shown him. So Sweet Medicine took the four arrows back to the Cheyenne tribe and told them the spiritual instructions he had learned from Maheo. He told the tribe of the power of the arrows, that they could defeat the evil that would come one day from white people who would go everywhere among the Indian lands. And he told the people they must obey the instructions and dance and pray to Maheo the Creator."

Redfeather paused. "You following this, Mama Courtney? You're awful quiet suddenly."

"Yeah, I guess. Sure is a nice story. I like the mountain part and the secret room. Is that why we're up here on this mountain now?"

"Yes, partly. And some of the stories say Sweet Medicine was accompanied to the mountain by a young woman, like maybe you, Mama Courtney. And afterwards they slept together so more Cheyenne would be born. Just like us on New Year's Eve, Mama. Making new Cheyenne! And that's a fine story too, but what's most important is that the Cheyenne always make the arrows as Maheo taught Sweet Medicine. And those arrows I use in my dance my mama, the daughter of a Cheyenne Medicine Man, gave me and she told me they were sacred, and that I must honor them. So I use them when I dance, and pray to Maheo. Only I don't have a tribe anymore, so I use them when I dance with my shadow, and just pretend we're a tribe. I just use those arrows in a way I hope pleases Maheo."

"Johnny," Amanda asked, "you believe those stories? I mean about the arrows coming from the creator in that mountain, and being, like you say, special and sacred?"

"Damn straight I do, Amanda! The old stories, what white people call I think legends, contain truth for Indian people. That's why we keep telling them to children. So they know Indian ways of thinking and living. That's why you and Mama Courtney are here. To learn. If we're gonna be a family, you all got to know about the Indian part of me, or at least what I can still remember of it. Now let's clean up here, and go down into the valley below this cabin and get us some berries and flowers, maybe make some tea for supper tonight."

"I reckon, Johnny Redfeather," Amanda said.

"And tonight when I dance at sundown, and then all the mornings and all the evenings while we are here on Raven Mountain, you all are going to dance with me. Just follow me. It's not hard. And we'll pray. "Hi-niswa' vita' ki' ni." That's Cheyenne for "We shall live again." And we will. All of us here. I'll teach you the words, and our little Indian will hear our prayers, and when he's born he'll already know some of our language. And we'll gaze at the stars, and try to figure out which ones Maheo has ordered to protect us."

"Johnny, that's a fine idea," Courtney said softly. "And maybe they'll even be a star just for our baby. Wouldn't that be really nice, Johnny?"

"I'll be all go to hell! It sure would be, Mama Courtney." And he leaned over and kissed her.

13
Green River Saloon

"Well, what a surprise to see you," Marilee remarked as Courtney and Amanda stumbled into Milly's saloon a week later. "Nobody was sure we'd ever see you two again. Seemed like Johnny Redfeather had kidnapped you both."

"We weren't exactly kidnapped, Marilee. More like invited us to stay without telling us where we were going. You ever slept two to a narrow cot with a man who thinks nothing about having to shoot rattle snakes at his front door? The man is mad for sure!"

"Well," laughed Marilee, "mad or not seems now like you and Johnny got something going on together. Seems he can't be all bad. Or least now you don't think so all the time."

"Yeah, well, not all the time. You're right, Marilee. But that damn cot in his cabin sure was narrow. Least my bed upstairs got room for two. Anyway, me and Amanda got to find a tub and some hot water. Milly around?"

"Yeah, she and Frank are out back. I'll go tell them you're here. Snuffy, how'd you like being with Redfeather? You been out with him twice now. Didn't you tell me he took you to Eagle Canyon a while back? And what's with this 'Amanda' now?"

"Yeah, we were at Eagle Canyon. Real pretty. His cabin's all right too. Johnny calls me Amanda now, and from now on that's my name, even here. Johnny told me Amanda was my Indian mama's name, and I like that much more than Snuffy."

"Well, that's a change. I'll be sure to tell everyone the news. Your mama was Indian? Funny, all these years Milly never said anything about your mama, who she was or where she came from. Guess she must have told Johnny, either that or he figured out more about you than we all did.

Well, I'll tell Milly and Frank you're here. She'll sure want to talk to you both. And I'd like to know what all you did up there with Redfeather for a whole week. What was it like?"

"Well," sighed Courtney, "he talked non-stop every night about Indian stories, and the animals up there, and Indian food, and some crazy monster he says lives up in the mountains. He 'bout scared me half to death every night. Almost as bad as the bears and what else he said were in the meadow and who knows where else? And every morning at sun rise, and again in the evening after supper, he was outside dancing around in a big circle, gesturing up and down and pointing at the four arrows he set up around the circle. Said it was something about a sun dance he remembers his mama taught him. After the first morning Amanda and I danced with him, and prayed some Cheyenne words he taught us. I don't guess the sun or the moon knows anyone's out there dancing around in circles and chanting Cheyenne words, but it was kind of beautiful. I liked it. Johnny said we were praying to Maheo, the Creator, and he said maybe Maheo would assign a star to protect our little Indian. Isn't that sweet? "

"I should say so," Marilee replied. "Yeah, I like that idea."

"So do I. Anyway, we can talk later. Amanda, come on up with me."

"Yes, Courtney. Warm water time."

As Courtney and Amanda headed up the stairs, Redfeather walked into the saloon carrying bedrolls and two large saddlebags. "Marilee, how you been? Glad to see you. You see the sheriff lately? He still come in here regular? Today's Saturday I figure, so seems he might be in here tonight."

"Yeah. Sheriff still comes by fairly often. Probably both him and his deputy be in here later. You got business with him, or just want a friendly visit with some whiskey?"

"Maybe a little of both, though I'm thinking maybe not so much whiskey anymore. Now if you would, please take this saddle bag back to Milly."

"Sure thing."

"There's some deer meat in there for the saloon. I just killed it yesterday, so it's still fresh. Maybe she can use it tonight. Thanks. Think I'll head up to Courtney, see how she's doing after our ride back down. It was windy and pretty cold."

"Johnny, what are you and she planning on now about your kid?

You gonna be here in Green River? You fixing on working here? Railroad? Loggers? Seems you got to be making some plans of some kind now."

"Marilee, I know that. Maybe that's part of what I want to talk to Sheriff Talbot about. Don't think the railroad wants an Indian working with them, even half a one. Especially after what happened up in Reiser Canyon. I sometimes ride out with this Jeb Carlson fella from Union Pacific to talk with Indians about their raids and the track laying gangs. Running Bear didn't like that I did that, said I spent too damn much time with white men. True enough. Hard to avoid, especially now. But maybe Sheriff needs some help, though I know his deputy Grogan is still with him. But I'll talk to him. Right now I'd best get on upstairs to see Mama Dillard. I'll be all go to hell but she didn't much like riding all that way up or especially down the mountain on a horse."

"Well, that's not exactly lady-like, Johnny. You got to give her that."

"Yeah, I know. You see Milly tell her I'd like to talk to her."

"For sure. See you later."

As Marilee stepped toward the back of the saloon with Johnny's saddlebag Sheriff Talbot and Butch Grogan entered. Marilee turned to face them, and smiled when she saw Talbot. "Well, looks like a good night for strangers. Sheriff, Butch, nice to see you both. You here for supper? Johnny Redfeather just handed me a whole saddlebag full of fresh deer meat. Might make a good meal if you've got time for Sam to cook it. Won't take but too long."

"Well, Marilee, that's very nice I must say. Sure, we got time, right Butch?"

"Whatever you say, Sheriff."

"Sure, we can wait. We're here for a while anyway. Usual Saturday night business I figure."

"Good. I'll tell Frank to get at it. Oh, and Johnny said to tell you he'd like to talk to you tonight if you've got time. He's upstairs with Courtney and, well, Amanda. No more Snuffy she's decided. Up in the mountains Johnny told her that was her Indian mother's name, so she wants to be called that from now on. I like that, really sweet. Anyway, he'll be down before too long I imagine."

"Sure, we can talk to him. Been a while anyway. Say Marilee, I'd, well, I'd like to talk to you later, maybe near closing. That all right?"

"Why sure, Gentleman Jim, if I may call you that. Whatever you say."

"Fine, I'll look for you, say, around eleven, or whenever Milly and Frank decide to close up."

"That'd be nice. I'll get on these dinner orders right away. Grab a table. See you later, Jim."

As Talbot and Grogan walked to a table, Redfeather bounded down the stairs at the far end of the saloon. "Sheriff," he shouted when he saw Talbot, "I got to talk with you tonight. Mind if I join you and Grogan?" he called across the room as he walked briskly toward them. "Won't take too long." As he approached Talbot, Redfeather extended his hand, which Talbot, somewhat surprised, grasped eagerly. Redfeather nodded to Grogan, who acknowledged his silent greeting.

"Johnny, last time I shook your hand was above Eagle Canyon. What's that, about two months ago, or thereabouts? Not a good time. We didn't talk much about a week ago here. Hardly exchanged a word as I recall. Didn't think after Eagle Canyon I'd be seeing you too much more. Where you been anyway? You up with Running Bear for a while? Where'd you go after he and what's left of his tribe left their camp?"

"Stayed with some Indians west of here, mostly Arapaho. Not too long. Some few Cheyenne. Not too friendly to a 'mixed-up' Indian, as they call me. So, I struck out, went up to Raven Mountain to a cabin that Running Bear told me about. Old hunting place he said. Been there mostly by myself. Hunting some. Way I like it. Anyway, mind if I sit down?"

"Oh, hell, of course not. Didn't mean to keep you standing. Butch, get us three beers, would you, then join us?"

"Sure, Sheriff. Be right back. Ah, Johnny, okay if I sit in here with you and the Sheriff?"

"Course it is. Don't mind one bit if you do."

Grogan nodded, then headed for the bar as Redfeather and Talbot sat down. "So, Johnny, what's on your mind? By the way, I hear you and Miss Dillard about to start a family. Or should I say, have already started? Congratulations are in order I'd say."

"Yeah, we've started all right. Thank you. That's part of what I wanted to talk to you about tonight. See, I can't exactly just ride around with some stray bunch of Indians any more, like I was doing up at Running Bear's for a while, or out hunting with a few other Cheyenne, or those Arapahos west of here. Being mixed, you know, I'm not much wanted. I mean even Running Bear did not completely trust me. So, ever since last September here at Milly's you know about my shooting ability, and I was just wondering if you could use some help. You know, kind of a deputy, at least while I'm here in town. I need to think about providing for Mama and our little Indian, and I need to get some work and a place somewhere near Green River. Don't know what Milly's going to say 'bout me bunking here long time with Mama Courtney, but I could maybe do some work for her too. Seems since last September she might want to return the favor, you might say, for me and the ladies keeping Tompkin's gang from running all over this place."

Sheriff Talbot leaned back in his chair just as Grogan returned with three beers and set them down on the table. "Thank you kindly, Butch. Much appreciated. Let's drink to Johnny Redfeather's return to Green River."

The three men clinked glasses, then drank. "Butch, Johnny here is wondering if we could use some help, maybe as a second deputy. I've been thinking maybe you could use some help with riding out to the cattle ranges, and maybe with some miners and loggers getting into Indian hunting areas back up in the canyon country. Seems there's still men up there can't keep off Indian land. Might have to bring one or two in for a spell in the jail. Maybe that would impress some of them. And I know Johnny sometimes rides with this Carlson guy who works for the railroad, trying to stop any more shooting. Might help if Johnny rode out there with a badge pinned on his shirt. So, what do you say? This all sound all right with you?"

"Well, hell yes, it sounds very good to me! I'd sure appreciate the help. A lot of those panners remind me of some of the herders who worked for Tompkin. Just plain mean. Carlson told me some months back that Johnny sometimes rode out with him to the track layers, but I hadn't seen Johnny with him. But it makes sense all right. Could mean you'd have some more help in town too."

"Yes, good idea. I'll wire Jack Garland, the marshal for Dakota Territory, see about making this official. I've got a badge for you back in the office. We'll figure out some sort of schedule. Oh, by the way, I heard from Garland about Jake Bulger. He was released from a Denver jail in December last year, after serving six months for trying to rob a bank. Garland's not sure, but he thinks Bulger headed west, or maybe south. So he probably lied to me and Colonel Swanson when he said a while back that he never worked for Tompkin. He could have been among those who attacked Running Bear in April. No way of knowing for sure. So, best be careful if you're ever around him. He might know you killed Tompkin, and might seek revenge. Just so you know, Johnny."

"Sheriff, I appreciate you telling me all this. Being part Indian, you know, especially after what happened up at Reiser, there's no way to know how many white men here are aiming at my scalp. Could be any one of Tompkin's herders know what I did. So yeah, I'll be careful. Now I'd better go find Milly. See about a bunk for a while. Deputy, much obliged for your understanding."

"Sure, Johnny. Any time," Butch responded as Redfeather stood and headed toward the back of the saloon. "Sheriff," Grogan began, "seems maybe we got another deputy just about the right time. So Jake Bulger lied. Besides not wanting to be tied to Tompkin's raid, what do you figure that means for Johnny? Seems there's no good place for him anywhere. Running Bear is gone, damn herders sure don't want him around. Railroad men maybe tolerate him for dealing with Indians sometimes, but they know they're taking Indian land and they know that Johnny hates them for doing that."

"Yeah, you're right, Butch. He's almost a lost man now. Maybe being a part time deputy will give him some sense of belonging in Green River. Maybe even pacify Courtney Dillard, which would be quite an accomplishment. Lord, that woman is a bundle. But maybe she's just what Johnny needs right now. A pregnant screech owl to hold his hand at night."

"Ha! Right! That she is," laughed Grogan.

Marilee approached their table with two plates of cooked deer meat and potatoes. "Well, Sheriff, Butch, here's that dinner you ordered. Frank said Sam cooked it just right for both of you. Hope it's done to your satisfaction."

"Well, Marilee, tell Frank and Sam that we appreciate their efforts. I'm sure it will be fine. Right, Butch?"

"Absolutely, Sheriff. Can't wait to dig in. Thank you, Marilee."

"Don't mention it. Glad to serve you both. Sheriff, perhaps I'll see you later. Hope so."

"Yes, Marilee. I'll come find you later this evening. Depends on how things are once this place fills up and gets busy. Never know around here on a Saturday night."

"Ha, don't I know that!" Marilee responded. "Till later. Butch, enjoy your stay. Hope it's peaceful."

"Much obliged, Marilee."

Marilee winked at Talbot as she turned and walked back toward the bar amid a growing chorus of calls for dinner and more spirits. "God, I hope someday 'Gentleman Jim' and I can walk out of this damn saloon and never return," she thought as Milly motioned her to the bar and asked her to deliver a tray full of two whiskey bottles and glasses to a group of increasingly impatient loggers. "Someday, someday," she thought.

§

Thirty minutes later Butch stood and pushed his chair into the table. "Sheriff, I'll walk around a bit, see what's happening over at that table of whiskey drinkers. Must be four bottles on that table by now. I won't be long."

"Okay. I'll wander over to the bar, see about Miss Marilee. See you later."

Sheriff Talbot stood and walked slowly toward the bar. Marilee saw him coming, then nodded her head toward the small nook further down and behind the bar. She stood within the secluded space, and when Talbot entered she grabbed him and kissed him passionately. "Tonight, Jim? Tonight?"

Talbot pulled back, and stared into her face. "Your eyes are really dark, beautiful, almost mysterious. I never really noticed them before."

"Well my my, aren't you the one with words tonight! That's right sweet. Not what most men in here first notice about me, that's for sure. But you haven't answered my question."

Talbot bowed his head and sighed deeply. Marilee lifted up his chin, then kissed him again, long and hard. "Suddenly lost for words? You started out real fine," she whispered. "Your eyes aren't bad either, now that I see them up close."

"Marilee, uh, I wanted to ask you, well, I thought I'd drive my buggy back into town tomorrow around noon, and then if you'd like we could drive back to my cabin for the day."

"And the night?" Marilee asked softly, a grin spreading across her face.

Talbot paused, and she grabbed his vest and pulled him to her yet again as hard as she could. "Jim, for the night also! We can have a night and a morning together. Just us two. Won't bother about anybody or anything else. Not the coyotes, the bears, the wolves, the...."

"The snakes?" Talbot chuckled, pressing his lips against her neck.

"Nope! Not even the damn snakes," Marilee giggled, as she lovingly stroked the back of his neck. He looked at her. "Right about noon then, outside Milly's."

"Right. Night and morning?"

"Night and morning!"

Talbot held her tightly, kissed her again, then gently pulled away. "Time to walk around for a spell. I'll look for you one more time before Butch and I leave."

"Always duty, isn't there? I'm thinking I might try getting used to that. Till later. You know where I'll be. For now, kiss me one more time like you mean it!"

"Maybe now I'll always mean it." He kissed her deeply while stroking her back and her hips, then slowly let go and walked back into the typical Saturday night turmoil of Milly's Green River Saloon.

§

Around nine o'clock Jeb Carlson hailed a blonde waitress named Suzanne. "Do me a little favor, Miss. Bring me a large whiskey. I'd be much obliged."

"Sure thing. Anything else I can get you?"

"Well, might just be a little something later on we could talk about. Whiskey's fine for right now."

"Sure thing. Room's number seven, in case you want to talk later. Whiskey comin' up!"

Carlson admired the sway of Suzanne's hips as she walked back toward the bar. "Must see about them later," he told himself. "Yes, indeed. So, Johnny Redfeather is back in town," he mused. "Best tell Bulger, like I said I would. But I wish to hell I knew that rebel's mind."

14
Jesse Smith's Bunkhouse

At noon two days later Jeb Carlson and Jake Bulger sat at a small table outside Jesse Smith's bunkhouse. Sitting hunched over the table, they whispered and avoided eye contact with the men hovering nearby.

"I saw him at Milly's Saturday night. So he is back in town, or at least he was then. He was talking to the sheriff and his deputy, but with the noise and shouting and crazy piano banging I couldn't make out what any of them said. I have no way of knowing how long he'll be here or where he's staying."

"Well, I appreciate knowing this much at least, Jeb. Like I said back at Hal's, we got a score to settle for my brother. War or no war, even if they were trying to escape Lawton, what they did to my brother was awful. He was just a kid! Seventeen! Don't see how that's justified. He didn't even have a gun, for Christ's sake! I just got to ask Redfeather why he did that, see if I can get a sensible answer."

"Jake, you and I both know there's nothing sensible in war. Some general puts a gun in your hand and tells you to shoot everything that moves over on the other side. All the blue coats. Just kill 'em! And don't ask why."

"Yeah, I know that right enough. So did Hank. But still...."

"Jake, find Redfeather and talk to him if you want. Ask him about that day back at Lawton. Ask him what the guards might have been doing to some of Swanson's men. Maybe knowing something about that might make you understand what Redfeather did. And maybe just talking now would do you more good than trying to avenge Hank's death. You can't bring him back, and you know that. No sense in more killing now, and remember: Redfeather and that sheriff spend time together. You kill Redfeather and you may have an angry sheriff on your tail."

"Jeb, let me worry about all that. Right now I just want to find that Indian, and we'll see what happens next. For now, thanks for telling me that he's back in town. Best let me be now."

Carlson rose to go, then stopped and turned back toward Bulger. "Don't forget, Jake, you yourself said Redfeather is a hell of a shot. Best be really careful."

"Yeah, for sure. I will be. Thanks again."

Carlson walked back to his horse, mounted, and rode swiftly toward Green River. Jake Bulger remained sitting at the table, his head down and his fists clinched. "You all right, Jake?" a herder asked him. Bulger looked up. "Yeah, I'm all right. I'm fine. I'm just fine. "

15
Raven Mountain Meadow

At one o'clock outside the Dakota Hotel several days later Redfeather watched as Swanson loaded two hunting rifles and a saddlebag full of food onto his horse. "I see you got my messages," Johnny said.

"Yeah, I got your messages Johnny. Thanks. Where'd you go anyway?" Swanson asked.

"I found this old cabin that Running Bear told me about up in an Indian hunting ground on Raven Mountain. He told me that Cheyenne used to hunt elk and deer up there. Bear even. I can't always stay at Milly's, though I'm there often enough now. I had to find a place to get away you might say. So I stay up there some now. Real peaceful. Only place I can be alone now when I need to be, which happens sometimes. I took Amanda and Mama Darla up there last week 'cause we all got lots to talk about. Haven't been any other white people up there except them. I'll be all go to hell but I don't want any other white folks visiting if I can help it, but I figure I can trust you, so's that's where we'll stay."

Swanson loaded the last of his saddlebags onto the back of his horse. "Well, you sure you want to take me up there? Lord knows we spent enough time during the war sleeping in those crummy bed rolls, or laid out under some tree somewhere. Could do that again I suppose."

"Well, let's mount and head out. We can ride toward Raven Mountain, then decide as we go along. It's early and going to be a damn hot day, so we can make plans as we ride. Let's go!"

Redfeather and Swanson mounted their horses. "You lead. Just like in Georgia. I'm just following you all day," Swanson added.

After a vigorous ride, they emerged from the forest into Raven Mountain Meadow less than two hours later. The mountain stared down on them, as if questioning their right to enter its domain. On the west-facing wall hanging glaciers glistened under the blazing late afternoon sun. From the highest ridge right down to the base, huge rocky arms spread before them. Redfeather stopped his horse just as the entire mountain came into view.

"Stop here a minute, Colonel." Johnny sat straight in his saddle, gazing at the mountain and its shimmering glaciers. "Big ole mountain, isn't it?" he boasted. "Just right for one Indian!"

"Johnny, you live up there? How the hell you get there, if you don't mind me asking?"

"Well, you can't see it from here, but there's, well, sort of a trail, out across the meadow and into the foothills and then up the south flank of the mountain. Steep, rocky. Need a damn good, strong horse that can pick its way around the rocks and that's also not afraid of Grizzly bears and the big cats that roam around and hunt in the meadow and up in the hills. Once you get higher there aren't any snakes. Not like Georgia, anyway you look at it."

"Snakes! Jesus, Johnny! Damn snakes still following you around? I'd have thought you'd had enough of them in Georgia."

"I have, but there's some here. Big rattlesnakes in this meadow, some up in the foothills. Lots for them to eat. Ha! Anyway, let's ride into the meadow. Maybe find a spot to bunk for the night. We got time, don't need to go all the way to the cabin today."

"You going to stand guard all night if we camp out here? You're a damn better shot than I will ever be."

"Well, maybe some. Let's see where we bunk in the meadow. Anyway, let's ride some. We go east now, toward the mountain. We can talk more later."

The tall grasses and wild flowers, bursting forth now in early June from under the remaining snow cover, brushed against their horses' legs, for several minutes the only sound marking their steady progress across the meadow toward the sage-covered foothills. As they rode, Redfeather remembered where Running Bear had camped deep in Reiser Canyon. "Like this once," he thought. "Peaceful. Quiet." Riding with a white man, even one he believed he could trust, toward the face of the mountain and the trail that led eventually to his cabin, Redfeather wondered if he might be making a fatal mistake. He knew that at the end of the war he was hated by both sides, and that he had killed so many soldiers and officers, Confederate and Union, that he could no longer trust any man who wandered into Green River. Every time he saw a stranger in Milly's he memorized the man's face and instinctively mistrusted him. Could be the brother, father, son of one of the many victims of his sharp-shooting, and he knew never to turn his back on a stranger. He had killed several of Swanson's men, and he knew that Swanson might never forgive him for those killings. Now leading Swanson slowly through this meadow that he cherished in its early summer bloom, Johnny O'Shaughnessy Redfeather, the half-Irish half-Indian gun-slinger who no longer felt welcome anywhere, wondered if he would ever again find the peace he sought so desperately.

"This will do," Johnny said as he stopped his horse about an hour later near a small stream and a clump of white pine trees. "Let's bunk here. Like old times. This meadow is spectacular, can't believe the stars at night. Bunch of Indian spirits go riding across the mountain skies every night. What do white men call them, constellations? Think that's right. Indians' spirits roam, play up there. I could show you. Running Bear's son for one. And Cheyenne spirits visit in these mountains too. Nonoma, thunder spirit, maybe Wihio, spider-trickster. Don't get too close to spiders out here. And maybe big Hestovatohkeo'o. Some Cheyenne stories say he's real, not just a spirit. I can't say for sure. Never seen him. But supposed to be a mean ole thing, monster-like. Got two faces, one of them deadly. You meet him up in these mountains or anywhere else, don't look at him. He'll try to trick you into staring at him, then he'll turn his head and his other face will kill you. Indians say the spirits, and especially Hestovatohkeo'o, don't like white men too much.

"Holy shit, Johnny, what the hell you planning for me out here? Don't any of them like white men?"

"Why the hell should they? Tell me that, why don't you? Won't do any harm now though. At least that's what I hope. Now let's set up, maybe get some grub. Have to take turns tonight with the food. We can maybe get it strung high enough in one of these branches. Aren't too many trees this high up, but there's a big pine over there just beyond the stream that might do. Grizzly bears wandering around, mountain lions be prowling tonight, wolves, coyotes. Got to be careful. We'll make the cabin tomorrow easy."

§

"That wasn't bad, Johnny. Where did you learn to cook?" Swanson asked later as they sat around the dwindling fire in the gathering dusk.

"Cook? I'll be all go to hell. I just slapped two of Milly's deer steaks in a pan and stuck 'em in the fire. Real easy."

"Well, it's sure a lot more tasty than what that cook at Milly's, Sam, has served me twice now. I recall now she, or maybe it was Roxy or Marilee, asked me if I could give Sam some pointers on cooking steaks. I said sure, but hell you could do that just as well. Maybe better for all that."

"Maybe. Maybe not. But thanks anyway."

"Sure, Johnny. Say, you haven't said much about yourself since we met at Milly's a while back. You said you survived running and hiding for two years, mostly with other Indians, till you got to Green River and these mountains. But not much else."

"Well, Colonel, being part Indian and part Irish, I don't really fit in anywhere now. I came up here after the war looking for Cheyenne, since my mama always told me they were her people, and after Sand Creek lots of Cheyenne chiefs left, scattered all over. So I came here, heard about Running Bear, went up to Reiser Canyon and stayed there for some time. But Running Bear never completely trusted me, said I spent too much time with white people. Said I was bad luck. I don't blame him, maybe I am. He didn't want me around too much, just sometimes. So I found this cabin that he told me about, started staying there. Fixed it up some. Also started coming to town, got to know a few white folks, Milly, Sheriff Talbot, Doc Johnson. I started drinking way too much whiskey at saloons, including Hal's, fuckin' too many white women, all kinds of crap like that. Well, after the killing, Running Bear left the canyon, took what few remaining braves, women, children he had. Went north I think, don't know where exactly, but he didn't want me along. So I stay mostly by myself in the cabin, come to town sometimes. Now lady Darla tells me I'm going to be a daddy, and so here comes another half-Indian, half-white kid, and suddenly I got to figure out a whole bunch of stuff about providing for a family. "

"What the hell, Johnny, how you figuring on doing that?"

"Don't rightly know yet. Most white people in town got little use for any Indian, even what they call a half-breed like me. Sheriff's got a good deputy already, Grogan, nice guy, but Talbot knows I can shoot fast and straight, like I did back in September at Milly's. Saved his life there, then did it again up at Reiser during the attack on Running Bear. I figure he owes me one, maybe two favors, and he agreed here some days back at Milly's that he could take me on as a deputy. Maybe a few days a week, something like that. Not sure how all that will pan out, but at least it's a start for me in town.

"Johnny, you going to raise Darla's kid out here? As an Indian? What does Darla think about all this?"

"Well, we had a little talk about that up at my cabin. That saloon is no place for any child that's got any Indian blood at all. Indians losing land, water, buffalo, god-damn fire wagon coming fast again, and most white people out here just as soon see us dead, figuring that way we can't bother all these 'settlers,' as they call themselves. Settlers! Hell, Indians settled these parts thousands of years ago. Who knows when exactly? Why white people call themselves 'settlers'? Shit! Worse god-damn nonsense I ever heard."

"Johnny, I'm sorry. Really, I am. I saw all this coming west after the war. Dead buffalo all along the train route. Outright slaughter. I...."

"It's not just buffalo. It's Indian people too!! Like up at Reiser Canyon, god-damn Sand Creek massacre. You must know about that. Black Kettle had a white flag run up. Chivington saw it. Attacked anyway. Killed hundreds. Whites are worse than Grizzly Bears, Mountain Lions, even snakes. Animals kill to eat, to survive. Ve'ho'e, white men, kill just 'cause they hate us, and sometimes I swear just for killing's sake! Cheyenne, all Indians, Epevo'eha, broken to pieces now, everywhere."

"Yeah, Johnny, I heard about Sand Creek all right. And I am truly sorry. Saying that does no damn good, I know, but here, right now, that's all I can do."

Swanson sighed, then lowered his head. For several minutes neither acknowledged the truth that Redfeather had spoken. Finally, Swanson picked up their tin plates and headed for the small stream. "I'll wash these pans, be right back."

Redfeather watched Swanson walk toward the stream. Again, the old doubt: could he ever trust any white man? Should he show Swanson the trail to his cabin, hidden now under dense prairie growth and higher up beneath the remaining layers of snow? Would the tracks from his ride there with Courtney and Amanda still be visible days later?

When he returned, Swanson placed some sweet candies on a plate and offered them to Johnny. "Johnny, here, have some. I bought these at Milly's little sweets shop down the street from her saloon. Lady clerk swore by them."

Johnny took several small pieces. "That's right kind, Colonel. Thank you."

"Sure, you're welcome. Least I could do."

For several minutes they sat quietly around the dying embers, sucking on pieces of peppermint candy. Raven Mountain, its gigantic glaciated wall bathed in the reddish-orange alpenglow of a serene summer evening, loomed over the now silent meadow.

Johnny looked east toward the glowing mountain. "Colonel, I killed a lot of your men before we got together. I know you know that. Course I didn't know they were yours at first, but I realized that once we talked at Lawton. It was war, I know, but still, given all that's happened since, I figure I should apologize...."

"Johnny, Stop! Pay that no mind! Like you said, it was war, and in war, you kill or you get killed. Simple as that. Whites have killed more Indians than I could ever count or apologize for. And like you said, it seems just for killing's sake. Like Chivington. Christ! Makes me ashamed sometimes to have worn that uniform, seeing as how I believed in what we fought for then. But that was then, and seems like everything is different now. Sure as hell I could never wear that uniform now."

"Yeah, I couldn't wear any damn uniform again either. Doesn't matter which one. Anyway, I just wanted to say that to you, before I forgot. Like you said, it was war. Anyway, gettin' cold. Let's get these bedrolls out of that saddle. I'll find some branches and rig this lean-to I brought, keep the dew off our blankets. I got all our food in a sack in my saddlebag, plus some rope. You string up the sack over on that big pine, and I'll get a little sleeping quarter set up here."

"Good idea. I'll be right back."

Thirty minutes later Swanson slid between a woven mat and a heavy wool blanket next to Redfeather. Already settled into his bedroll and lying on his back, Johnny gazed at the trillions of lights appearing above him, taking over one part after another of the heavens that the sun had abandoned. "Suppose there's Indians up there, Colonel? Maybe running buffalo forever among all those stars, just riding and riding wherever the buffalo roam? And never feeling lost, never thinking the prairie's going to end, or some white men are going to run them off what they call 'their land'"?

"Suppose that's possible, Johnny. Awful lot of room up there for sure. Damn cold though. Speaking of which, think I'll fold this blanket around me and try to doze."

Redfeather chuckled. "Last time you and I slept together in the same room was back in Lawton Prison. I figure this is much better. Not so crowded. Air doesn't stink like it did back there either."

"Ha! You're right on both points, Johnny. This meadow sure is peaceful. Couldn't see any stars at all inside that prison. Say, what about the wild cats and grizzly bears you mentioned? Will they come snooping around here?"

"Maybe, but chances are good I'll hear any visitors. You got the food up high?"

"Yeah I did. Tied a rock around one end of the rope, slung it over a high branch. No bear or cat will get our food. Now if you'll pardon me...."

"Sure thing, Colonel. Good night."

"Good night, Johnny."

Redfeather lay awake for several minutes, listening carefully to the wilderness for signs of either the grizzly sow he knew was somewhere in this meadow, or the mountain lions that prowl this territory at night. He remembered that, after the raid on Milly's, he had retreated to a corner of the saloon and sat down at a small table where, after several minutes, he had succumbed to the alcohol and laudanum that provided him some solace, some peace. He had wondered then, as he wondered now, where and how he might find a place where he belonged among other men. The thought of thousands of Indian braves riding high and free amid the exploding stars gave him hope that such a place might still be found, even here in these mountains. And with that hope he slipped into sleep.

16
Hunters

Next morning Redfeather was up first. As he rolled out of his bedding a large raven, perched high on a white pine near the stream, cried raucously into the still, grey light of the emerging dawn. "Complaining again, are you?" Johnny thought. "Damn ravens think they can tell the sun when to rise. It's coming, Mr. Raven, but it will just take its own sweet time, just like yesterday and just like tomorrow. No one tells the sun what to do." Self-assured of his philosophy, Redfeather walked to the tree where Swanson had hung their food the night before, took down the sack, then walked back to their campsite and started a fire from last night's embers. As the first glint of sunlight peeked over the highest ridge on Raven Mountain, Redfeather looked back at the raven still trying to command the sun. "Told you it would come," Johnny said to the bird. "Just stop all that chatter why don't you? Does no damn good at all!" The raven replied with an angry shriek.

Johnny had coffee made and bacon frying over a fire before Swanson rolled out from under his wool blanket.

"Morning Colonel," Johnny greeted Swanson as he groaned and peered out at him. "I don't quite remember you sleeping so long back in the war. What's gotten into you?"

"Age, Johnny, age," Swanson mumbled. "These old bones aren't quite what they were even a few years ago. Don't tell me you haven't experienced that."

"Indians don't have time to let their bones grow old. Too many white men and soldiers chasing them. Don't have time to stop and let their bones get rusty. Got to keep moving!"

Colonel Swanson roller back under his blanket. "Coffee smells damn good, Johnny. Just give me five more minutes before I have to get up and face the day. My bones are not only getting old, they are cold!"

"Cold? Colonel, I'll be all go to hell but you really are getting soft. Was never this way in the war. Not what I recall."

"Johnny, white men's bones get older and colder faster than Indians'. Soon as I get a little warmer I'll be up and fine." A few seconds later Swanson suddenly yelled, "There!" as the sun exploded over Raven Mountain and struck the east-facing opening of the lean-to. "Damn smart construction, Johnny," Swanson exclaimed as he rolled over to face the sunlight that immediately warmed him. "You obviously know this meadow and that mountain well. Suppose the entrance to this cabin of yours up on that mountain faces east too, right?"

"Yep," Redfeather said, and returned to flipping the bacon frying on the pan. "This bacon about done, Colonel. Best get up before I eat every scrap of it."

Swanson crawled out of the heavy blanket, then stood up facing the sun. "This mountain sure beats those we ran through in Georgia. Those were just hills compared to this monster. This whole country is just huge, Johnny."

"Yeah, well, that's how Indians out here like it. Big and open. We used to think there were enough mountains and canyons to wander in forever. Not quite true anymore, but some places still mostly for Indians. This one, Eagle Canyon, a few others."

"Yes, seems the whole country is coming west, and everybody wants the same land. But right now, standing here in this sunlight, all I can think about is that coffee and bacon you've prepared. It's too early for anything else."

"Well, if you say so, Colonel. But hard for Indians not to think about that. Anyway, let's eat."

§

As they rode east across the meadow toward the foothills Redfeather pondered again his decision to lead Colonel Swanson to his cabin. Although Courtney Dillard and Amanda had already stayed there for several days, he now thought of them as his family. But a white man, even one he had fought beside in the Civil War and helped escape from prison, seemed very different. He wanted to believe that he could trust Swanson, but he also realized that Swanson could not conceive his lingering anxieties.

He also feared the tracks their horses left in the snow—even in June—as they steadily climbed the steppes that, resplendent with fresh sage, unfolded before them as they rode toward hunting grounds on the southern flank of the mountain. Redfeather knew that these snows would not completely melt for nearly another month, maybe longer. Despite the lack of tree cover their tracks would remain along most of the higher elevations of the trail and well into summer behind the crest of the mountain where the sun shone for only a few hours each morning. A true sanctuary, he wondered? Or another Reiser Canyon, fatally discovered by white men?

An hour's ride brought them to a field of boulders strewn around the lower foothills by one of the mountain's colossal glacial falls. Redfeather knew the dangers of the glaciers hanging thousands of feet above them. Seemingly at will, the mountain released its hold on gigantic slabs of ice and rock that cascaded down the west-facing cliffs at unimaginable speeds, crushing everything below. He knew not to antagonize Raven Mountain, lest it unleash its thundering fury on him and whomever he dared bring into its forbidding sanctuary. He prayed to Maheo that Raven Mountain would accept the white man traveling with him to hunt its creatures.

Just to the left of the boulders was a clump of sub-alpine fir trees, and here Johnny told Swanson to tether his horse. "The elk and deer come here to nibble on the leaves and the grasses. There's a small stream that runs just before the trees, and the animals come there to drink. We can take cover here, use it like a blind, and probably be able to get us a couple nights' supper. We just have to be patient, that's all. I'm praying Raven Mountain will be good to us, send us some of its wild things to feed us while we're visiting here."

"Johnny, you don't actually pray to this mountain, do you? I mean it doesn't listen. It's just a huge hunk of rock. Right?"

"Hell yes I pray to the mountain! Indians know how to pray to the earth and everything on it. Mountains, trees, rivers, rocks. Not just a huge hunk of rock and ice. The mountain will let us know if it's listening and what it wants to say in return. Just listen." Johnny dismounted, tied his horse to a pine tree next to Swanson's, then walked to an opening between two huge round boulders and crouched down, his rifle lying beside him. "Come sit down here with me. This spot's good as any for hunting deer and elk. Maybe bear too, though I'd prefer not to eat bear if we don't have to. Not much good I'd say."

"I've never eaten bear, I must say," Swanson replied.

"Well, I hope we don't have to," added Johnny. "Pretty sure we'll get us at least one deer. Lots of them around this meadow this time of year. Just got to be patient."

Swanson sat down next to Redfeather and laid his rifle against a rock. "You seem to know this country well. These foothills sure are pretty. Hell of a wild place too I'd say. You been hunting up here much?"

"Yeah, lately I've been up here often. It's peaceful, you know. No white people up here, except Amanda and Mama Dillard like I told you. Least ways not yet. You'd be the first white man I've ever had at the cabin. That's all right with me. I just got to hope it's all right with the mountain."

"Johnny, how exactly are we supposed to know that? I mean we're sitting right below it, looking up at those mean glaciers, all rock and ice. Doesn't look real inviting I must say."

"We'll know. The deer or elk will tell us. Just be patient now."

Redfeather brushed aside a layer of snow and laid down a wool blanket he had removed from his saddle. He and Swanson settled into comfortable positions on a bed of thick grass. The sun had by now risen high over Raven Mountain, and caressed the multi-colored meadow below them. The morning air, still noticeably chilly at higher elevations, gradually warmed. Overhead an eagle drifted majestically on the warm rising air, like the hunters searching for sustenance from the mountain's bounty. Cumulous clouds drifted lazily over the mountain, their ragged shadows painting large sections of the shimmering glaciers a darker hue. The men sat quietly for several minutes, just gazing at the landscape and relishing the sun on their backs.

"This meadow is certainly peaceful, Johnny. Nice warm sun, clear day. Sure beats Georgia."

"For sure, Colonel. Why I come up here alone. Just me and the mountain, and whatever it decides to send my way. "

"That creature, or whatever it is, two-face, I think you called it. You figure he's really up here somewhere?"

"Hestovatohkeo'o?"

"Yeah, that one. What the hell is it, some kind of huge bear?"

"Well, not sure what it is, a real body or a mythical spirit, or where it is at any one time. Never seen it. But our stories say it walks on two feet, a giant, black, man-like thing. Cheyenne elders insist it's real, not just a spirit from ancient myths. Some say they've seen him in these mountains and even down in the canyons. Spirits, though, are always around, but of course you can't see them. Guess that's the point of being a spirit."

"Yeah," sighed Swanson, chuckling and clearing his throat. "Guess that'd be the case all right."

Redfeather laughed. "Colonel, Indians know to believe. They have to have something, or someone, to believe in. Especially now."

"Yes, I can see that, Johnny." They sat silently, waiting. Fifteen minutes later a deer appeared to their left in a clearing about twenty-five yards away. Redfeather stood, aimed, and fired. The deer dropped immediately. "Didn't suffer, not one bit," Johnny said as they moved out of the clearing toward the slain animal. "Guess Raven Mountain wanted to be good to us today, Colonel," Redfeather said as he knelt beside the deer. "Got us a couple of nice steaks here, maybe three or more. Let's get this up onto my horse, and head out. Still got a ways to ride today, and it's all uphill. I'll skin it tonight, cut up some good pieces of nice fresh meat. Wolves and cats can have the scraps."

"Sure thing, Johnny. I'll go get the horses." As Swanson walked back to the boulders, Johnny, still kneeling, looked at the mountain towering above him. Its two massive arms reached toward him, as if embracing him, offering shelter in its fierce, forbidding wildness. "I thank you, Raven Mountain. I honor this gift. The white man and I shall not waste it, but shall use it to strengthen our bodies and mend our hearts."

"Come on Colonel," Redfeather said when Swanson returned. "Help me get this deer on my horse. We got to get up this long, steep trail before dark. Don't want scavenger mountain lions, wolves, or any damn coyotes trying to steal our dinner. And the snow's going to get deeper the further up we go."

"Yes sir! Lead the way!"

§

Swanson and Redfeather sat on the wide step below the front door of the cabin. The golden rays of an early summer sunset stretched across the sky, lingering, as if reluctant to relinquish to night's clutches its celestial brilliance.

"Johnny, you should have been a cook in that lousy war. Butchered, skinned, cooked, and served. Seemed to take no time at all. Done just right, I must say."

"Why thank you, Colonel. Spend any time up here, especially alone, you got to have all sorts of what the army called 'survival skills.' Either that or starve. Besides, Indians are used to living in the wild, hunting, fishing, cooking what they get. All that time with the buffalo, you know. Whites like to call us 'savages,' but we're just surviving our way. Always been that way with us."

"Yeah, I see that all right. A whole way of life, isn't it? The buffalo, the deer you shot, elk, eagles. Raven Mountain. Right beautiful up here. I can see why you come here and fixed up this place."

"Colonel, I got just about no other place to go any more. Deer and elk got places to roam, but I don't. After the attack on Running Bear I took Sheriff Talbot to Eagle Canyon, told him it was one of a few remaining places for Indians that no white men had destroyed. Not yet anyway. Told him it was sacred to Indians, and I think he understood that. I took Amanda there because she's part Indian, and someone else around here has to know what that canyon means to Indian people in case I'm gone. After Reiser, no telling how many men from Tompkin's herders want me dead since I slit his throat and saved the sheriff."

"Johnny, I sure am sorry about Reiser. Seems now there's no need for more killing. But I guess I was wrong about that. Maybe peace is not possible out here either. Seems everyone is just out for taking whatever they want, never mind who was here first, or how they lived."

"That's about it all right. Who was here, and how they lived. No telling what future Indians might have, even way out here in these mountains. That's why I figure I have to get to Amanda now, and see about Mama Darla's little Indian growing inside her tummy. I got to figure out what to do about that child before it's too late."

"Well, Johnny, if I'm here long enough, maybe I can help in some way. Never know what one old soldier can do for another."

"Well Colonel, that's right nice of you. Nea'ese, thank you. I'll remember that. I don't hear a forked tongue when you speak. Guess being in a war together, getting captured, then escaping together does make us brothers under the skin." Redfeather reached out his right hand, Swanson grabbed his forearm, and then Johnny did likewise.

"Good!" Redfeather said, still holding Swanson's arm. "Arm-in-arm, brothers under the skin. I'll be all go to hell. Not just soldiers, brothers! Like Cheyenne say, Hoovehe, friend! Nepehevehetaneve, you're a good man!"

Swanson held Redfeather's arm several seconds more before releasing it. "I sure appreciate this, Johnny. I'll try to honor that gesture. I don't understand your words, but I will honor what you are saying."

"I'm sure you will. Speaking as one friend to another, Sheriff told me something last week you should know. This fella Jake Bulger, who you said also wants to take you hunting, lied to him about when he started working for Tompkin. A federal marshal told Talbot that Bulger got out of jail in December last year and may have come up here, so he might have been working for Tompkin when his herders attacked Running Bear. Don't know for sure he was, but good bet he was. I can see why he'd lie to Talbot about being at Reiser, but still, liars are never good to be around. I know nothing more about him, but Sheriff says be careful around him."

"Well, he sure wouldn't admit that he was with the attackers. But still, you're right about liars. Downright scum!"

"Yeah they are!" Redfeather agreed and looked over his left shoulder. "Well Colonel, the sun's heading down the mountain, and it's going to get cold up here in a hurry. I got to get out my arrows too before dark, so best get on with it."

"Arrows? What arrows?"

"Sacred Cheyenne Medicine arrows. Maahote. Got to put them out for a while while there's still some light. Got to dance a little and pray a bit to Maheo, the Great Spirit, asking for blessings. Won't take too long. I'll get them and get on with it. The bedrolls are inside, maybe you can set them on the cots. I won't be too long."

"Sure thing, Johnny, I'll do that," Swanson said as both men stood and walked into the cabin.

Redfeather emerged a few minutes later with his arrows and walked to the small stone ring at the center of the larger circle. He knelt for a few minutes, prayed to Maheo, then rose and walked to the outer circle. He removed the arrows from their sack, and, as he walked around the circle he placed one of the red-painted arrows pointing north and one south, and one of the black-painted arrows pointing east and one west. He walked the circle several times, touching each of the arrow heads as he passed it, then returned to the inner stone ring and knelt again. "Oh

Maheo, protect at least the Indian part of this man. Hi-niswa' vita' ki' ni," he chanted several times. Then he rose, walked once more around the circle, collected the arrows, and walked back into the cabin.

"Johnny, what was that little ceremony about?" Swanson asked.

"Well, what I know about Cheyenne ceremonies I heard from my mama in Florida. She told me about the Sun Dance, and how warriors walked in a circle around a pole inside an earth lodge or maybe out in a field. The whole tribe celebrated the dancers, she said. I saw one, Arapaho, when I was heading north after the war. It's a beautiful thing for the whole tribe, but I got no tribe now, just my shadow when I dance in the morning. So I ask Maheo to protect me and my shadow. Like we are a whole tribe, you know?"

Swanson stood silently for several seconds, then lowered his head and sighed. "I see, Johnny. Well, I hope the Great Spirit as you say protects you. And as I said a while back, I will help if I can."

"Right kind of you, again. Now let's close up this little cabin to keep the bears, coyotes, wolves, and cats out of here. It's getting cold and dark fast."

Swanson slumbered soundly. Across the room, Redfeather wondered again if by bringing Swanson to Raven Mountain he had incurred Maheo's wrath? Only when he accepted that he could not know did he succumb to sleep.

§

Early the next morning Johnny Redfeather again knelt in the stone ring and prayed to Maheo. Again he placed his arrows around the outer circle and began his ritual dance around the perimeter. Swanson watched in amazement from the cabin door, seeing a part of Redfeather about which he had known nothing. During the war he had experienced Redfeather's ferocious determination to remain alive and his amazing shooting ability, but he had neither seen nor believed possible the profound spiritual element of his character. "Surely," Swanson thought as he watched Redfeather move around the circle, "here is a man who believes in a world about which I know nothing. Surely he deserves to live."

"We'll hunt for one more day," Redfeather said an hour later after finishing a plate of bacon and beans that Swanson had prepared. "Maybe try to get us an elk this time. Damn good eating. Thanks."

"You're welcome. It was my turn. We hunting up here, or lower down the mountain?" Swanson asked.

"We'll go back down. Elk like the meadow in spring. Plus there they can see the mountain lions better, have more room to run if need be. Every animal likes the meadow now. Snakes too," Johnny laughed, remembering Swanson's fear of them in the Georgia swamps. "But we won't pay them any mind. Just look for a big buck. We'll have good eating tonight too, plus I'll take some meat down to Milly. I use it to pay my way at her saloon, you might say. I bring her fresh deer or elk and she usually lets me stay with Mama Courtney. That way I got a place to bunk when I'm in town. I like being here all right, but now I got to see about Courtney and our little Indian."

"You figure working as a deputy for Sheriff Talbot will be a part of that?"

"Well, yeah, Sheriff said he could hire me on, maybe just part time for now, but maybe he'll give me enough work eventually. I got to have something in town, but Mama and me and the little one going to have time up here too, in this Indian country. I'm figuring Amanda will be here some too. Her mama was Indian, so I got to care for her, teach her right. Can't let her grow up in that saloon. That's not a fit life for an Indian girl."

"No, I can't imagine it would be. Like I said, if I can help...."

"Well, and like I said I'll remember that. Just have to see what happens later. For now, let's finish and saddle up, get on down the mountain to the meadow. Some big buck down there is just waiting to provide us some fine meat. We'll bunk here again tonight, then head back to town tomorrow."

"That sounds fine, Johnny. Just fine."

17
Green River Saloon

"Well it's about time you got back here, Daddy Redfeather. Where the hell you been anyway?" Courtney Dillard yelled from the top of the stairs when she saw Redfeather and Swanson enter Milly's saloon late the following afternoon. "I had no idea where you been or when you were planning on returning. Don't you ever tell folks what you're up to?"

"Now Darla," Redfeather replied, amazed at her ability to appear suddenly, and loudly, seemingly from nowhere, "don't go getting your feathers all up in a bunch. I told Milly that Colonel Swanson and I were heading out for three days of hunting up in the mountains, and I thought maybe she'd tell y'all that. Seems like she didn't get around to telling you."

"No she didn't! Now git on up here quick! And stop calling me Darla!"

"I'll be there after I give this elk meat we brought to Milly. Hold onto your britches!"

Upon hearing Johnny's voice, Milly walked out from the back room. "Well Johnny, Colonel Swanson, welcome back. How was the hunting?"

"Just fine, Milly," Johnny responded. "We bagged a deer and a big elk, so we got some real good meat all cut up and wrapped just for you strapped to the back of our horses. Guess we can take it round back, right? Frank or Sam back there?"

"Yeah, Frank and Sam are both back there, getting ready for tonight. Saturday you know. Sheriff will be here too, least I hope so. This last week while you and the colonel were out hunting he and Marilee been spending some time together, so to speak. I suspect I'm going to lose her if this keeps up. Maybe have a wedding up at the church pretty soon, that's if Reverend Simpson will even let us in the front door. He still thinks we're all lost souls in here, though I guess he's quit trying to shut us down. By the way, what you planning on doing about Courtney? Seems some of my girls might not be working here too much longer."

"Well, I talked to Sheriff Talbot about being a deputy for a while, earn some pay, maybe get a place here for me and Darla. Amanda too. Plus we'll be up in my cabin on Raven Mountain some of the time. For now, I'll take the elk out back, then I better get on up to Darla. Don't want her screaming all over the saloon for me."

"No you don't. And I sure don't want that either. Guess we'll have to talk on all this later."

"Sure thing, Milly. Colonel, let's get that elk meat off our horses and carry it back to Frank."

"Yeah, good. I want to get back to the hotel. Get into a tub of hot water and wash some of this mountain grit out of my bones. Like you said, maybe I'm getting soft. Maybe I'll wander back here later."

§

At six o'clock that evening Johnny Redfeather, Sheriff Talbot, and Colonel Swanson sat at a table sipping whiskey and waiting for the elk steaks they had ordered almost an hour earlier.

"You shot it yesterday, that right Johnny?" Talbot asked.

"Yeah I did. Right fresh. Actually Colonel bagged it. Damn good shot I'd say. Just one bullet, right to the head. Elk didn't have time to suffer. The mountain was kind to us I'd say."

"Johnny prayed to it every night. Guess that helped. Right Johnny?"

"I'll be all go to hell, of course it helped!"

Talbot smiled at Johnny's emphatic remark, but Swanson's glare told him not to laugh. "I'm sure, too," Talbot added.

The ensuing silence was broken by Doctor Mark Johnson's "Hello" as he strode toward their table. "Doc," Talbot cried as he rose to shake his hand, "welcome. Lucky you're here. Have I got a surprise for you! Look who's sitting at our table!"

Swanson rose, and as he turned toward the entrance of the saloon, Johnson exclaimed, "What the hell? Am I seeing a ghost? Colonel William Swanson? Is that really you? When...? Oh for heaven's sake! What, when.... I just can't believe my eyes! I thought you had been killed near the end of the war."

"Well, believe them, Doctor Johnson, I'm standing right in front of you! Come here Mark and let me give you a good old-fashioned hug. You sure were valuable in those last months. Can't recall the last time we saw each other. Maybe early sixty-five, near the end? Johnny here must have heard the same story. Can't quite figure where that originated, but I sure am glad it was wrong."

"Yes, that's about right," Johnson said as he and Swanson eagerly embraced. "I left for Virginia I think in March of sixty-five. Never went back down south after that. I couldn't bear to do that after that insane war."

"Yeah, insane is a good word for war," Swanson replied. "I'll take that. Anyway Doc, have a seat. We got some serious celebrating to do. Agreed Sheriff? Johnny?"

"Hell yes, Doc! Join us," Talbot said. Before sitting down Johnson reached across the table to greet Johnny Redfeather. "Well, Johnny, and how are you? Haven't seen you in a while either."

"Well, Doc, I'm mostly up in a little cabin on Raven Mountain now, way up above the big meadow. Keepin' to myself."

"Ah, sure, Johnny, I understand," Johnson said quietly. "Still, nice to see you again."

"Likewise!"

"So, William," Johnson began, "last September Sheriff and I heard a rumor here in town that some drunk firing off his gun in Georgia had killed you. Johnny heard the same story."

"Yeah we did Doc," Redfeather said. "Guess now we'll never know where that came from."

"Well, so much for rumors," Swanson laughed.

"Agreed there, Colonel. Anyway, really glad to see you again," Johnson added.

"Doc, sit down and have a drink and some supper with us," Talbot said. "We'll see about ordering another plate. By the way, Doc, where you been lately?"

"Well, Jim, I've been delivering babies and trying to save snake-bite victims in a small community up river about three miles away. Had a real difficult delivery with one of the women. Kept me up most of the night. Thought the kid would never arrive. Thank goodness Maria was with me. So," Johnson added, turning to Swanson, "you plan on being here for a while?"

"Well, not sure about that yet. Just found Johnny here after we both thought the other had died in the war. So right now I'm just enjoying Johnny's company again and swapping old war stories. Been hunting with him up in Raven Mountain too. Just got back earlier today."

"Raven Mountain?" exclaimed Johnson. "That's one big, beautiful mountain. Never been up there, but it looms large from town here."

"Damn straight," responded Johnny. "Nice and peaceful up there too at times. Real good place to be alone, especially for Indians. Not too many places like that left out here."

"Yeah, I understand that all right," said Johnson. " Johnny, I sure hope you can find some place to feel at home around here. Can't be easy, though."

"You're right there, Doc," Johnny replied. "That little cabin, and maybe a few days here with Darla, er Miss Courtney Dillard, and her little Indian coming on, about all I got right now."

"Little Indian! Johnny, you telling me what I think you're telling me? A little Indian!"

"Sure enough, Doc. Darla and I might need you some four months from now. Never know how these things might go."

"Well," added Johnson, "I guess congratulations are in order, Papa. Here's to you!" Johnson replied, raising his hand. "Say, how can a man get a whiskey glass around here?"

"I'll get you one, Doc," Johnny replied. "Be right back. I'll see about our dinners too. Anxious to taste that elk me and Colonel brought back to Milly's today."

"Say Sheriff," Swanson began as Johnny headed to the bar, "while we were up in Raven Mountain Johnny told me that you had heard from a marshal that this Jake Bulger character lied to you about when he started herding with Tompkin. Johnny said that might mean he was among the attackers in Reiser Canyon. I ask because a while back here in Milly's, as you recall, Bulger invited me to go hunting with him, and today at the hotel there was a note from him inviting me again. Now I don't know whether I should accept his invitation or not."

"Well, Colonel, just because he lied about when he started herding for Tompkin doesn't mean he was part of the attack at Reiser Canyon. Doesn't mean he wasn't either. Maybe he's just trying to hide some history we don't know about. Maybe in the war, for instance. That's true of a hell of a lot of men out here now. If you enjoy hunting, I'd say go, but just be really careful. And remember what you just heard Johnny say about his sense of peace up on Raven Mountain. No need to mention that if you go anywhere near there."

"Yes, Sheriff, I heard that, and Johnny did talk about trying to find some peace somewhere he thought he still belonged. I understand that, and you know, even in the war he seemed lost at times. Hell, he started with the rebels. After he killed those guards at Lawton and we escaped, he just split again, all on his own. Said he'd go find what was left of Indian settlements on the way north, back to the Cheyenne he hoped. Craziest man I ever met."

"You know Bill, when you told me that story down in Georgia I had a hell of a time believing it at first," Johnson said. "Didn't seem possible. Guess I underestimated Johnny Redfeather, which I sure won't ever do again. No one alive should do that!"

"Yeah, and the dead sure as hell don't!" chuckled Talbot.

"Right you are, Jim," Swanson replied. Just then Redfeather returned with a glass full of whiskey, and handed it to Johnson. "Why thank you, Johnny! And here's to your new little one. Health and prosperity," Johnson exclaimed.

"Yes, for sure," Talbot said, and they all raised their glasses. "Thank you kindly," Johnny responded.

"Bill," Talbot began after they had sipped their whiskeys, "you ever get to know anyone in that Georgia prison? Any guards? Anyone who might hold a grudge against you both for escaping the way you did?"

"Why do you ask, Jim?" Swanson replied.

"Well, I am still bothered by Bulger's lying to me. And some weeks ago he invited you to go hunting when he didn't even know you. Just seems a bit odd, that's all. If Bulger was at Reiser Canyon he might know that Johnny killed Tompkin, and that might make him want to seek revenge. But why, Bill, would he want to take you hunting?"

"Well," Johnny suddenly interrupted, "I killed several guards that night, and slit a young guy's throat. I was cutting Swanson's hands free, and this guy grabbed me from behind. Knife was quicker than a gun. I didn't take time to shoot him, just let him bleed to death. I had no sympathy for what those guards were about to do with those prods."

Redfeather's retelling of that night in Georgia silenced the men. "Guess that's about as barbaric a story of that war as I've ever heard,"

Talbot remarked quietly. "Doc told us all about it the night of the raid on Milly's here."

"Sure is," responded Johnson. "Exactly why I came out here afterward. Thought I could get away from all that brutality. Say, who's this Bulger character?"

"He now herds for Jesse Smith," Talbot responded. "He told me one night in here that he didn't begin working for Smith until after the raid on Running Bear. Yet he knew the raid had been in Reiser Canyon, though he insisted he had heard that from one of Tompkin's men."

"Colonel," began Johnson, "after what I saw at Reiser Canyon I would not trust anyone who might have worked for Tompkin. Why'd he offer to take you hunting anyway?"

"I don't know for sure. That night he just came over to our table and offered to take me after he heard me talking to Jim about wanting to do some hunting in these parts. Just seemed really friendly at the time."

"Bill, you may be entirely right about that," Talbot added. "Maybe I am just being too concerned. But Mark here, and Johnny too, know that I trusted Tompkin one day too many, and look what happened! I am trying real hard not to make that kind of mistake again."

Just then Roxy and Marilee appeared carrying plates brimming with elk steaks and potatoes and placed them down on the table. "Doc, Johnny assumed you'd want to eat also so he asked us to add a dinner plate for you. Hope you like it."

"Well, that's very kind. Thank you! I'm sure it will be fine, especially since I hear Johnny and Bill delivered it just today. You know, Bill, that awful story about Lawton really is what prompted me to come west. Just leave the killing behind, I imagined. Hasn't quite worked out that way though, I must say."

"Sure hasn't for Indians!' Johnny proclaimed. "And I'll be all go to hell but we were here first! Anyway, for now let's enjoy this elk dinner. Fine gift from the mountain, don't y'all think?"

"Sure is, Johnny, and Doc and I thank you and William," Talbot said.

Except for occasional compliments about the elk meat, and even some for Sam's cooking, the men continued their meal in silence. When they had finished, Doc Johnson offered to buy another round of drinks. "Doc, I appreciate that, but if y'all will excuse me, I think I had better get on up to Mama Courtney Dillard before she starts screaming at me again from the top of the stairs. Woman can make a terrible racket when she has a mind to. I wouldn't want to inflict that on folks I consider friends. So I'll be off. Much obliged for the company." Redfeather rose and extended his hand to Swanson. "Colonel, good trip I'd say. Let's do it again some time."

"Yes, Johnny, we shall. Do say hello to Courtney for me," Swanson said as he rose and shook Redfeather's hand.

"I sure will, if I can get in even two words. Doc, enjoyed sharing a meal with you. Maybe see you again soon, in case Darla needs some help with our little Indian. Sheriff, maybe sometime soon we can talk about that deputy business. I'd sure appreciate that."

"We will, Johnny. Say, early next week. Town's pretty quiet recently, and Grogan's got a little place of his own now, so come by my office at the jail some morning. We'll see what I can do."

"For sure, Sheriff," Johnny said, nodded to Johnson and Swanson, and headed for the stairs just as Courtney Dillard appeared at the top of the landing. "'Bout time I'd say! Why some things take you so long and others are so damn quick I do not understand. Git up here!"

"I'm comin', Mama, I'm comin'. Be nice now. Not all that hard, really."

Swanson watched Johnny ascend the stairs two at a time, then shook his head. "Jim, Mark, I just spent three days with Johnny up in Raven Mountain, first hunting in the meadow, then two nights in his cabin way up on that huge mountain, tucked in a valley between two peaks. Damn beautiful place I'll have to admit. But Johnny's not the same man I remember. From what I've heard about Reiser Canyon I can understand why he's hurting inside, but he's awful lonely right now, and that's not good for any man. Seems he has nowhere to go, no place he feels is his, except for that mountain, and that's just terrible lonely and dangerous up there."

"William," replied Johnson, "I've known Johnny Redfeather for several years, including some down in Florida before we all headed west. Because he's mixed, you know, Irish and Indian, he just can't seem to fit in anywhere. I remember at Sandy Bluff last fall, when Sheriff Talbot, Johnny, and I met with Running Bear. Johnny said Running Bear told him that he spent too much time with white men. And since Johnny is still here I'm assuming that when Running Bear left Reiser Canyon with what was left of his tribe, he told Johnny he was not wanted. So, where does he go now? I do not know."

"Well," replied Swanson, "I'd say he goes into himself and his spirits, whoever they be. He had a little ceremony up at his cabin with some arrows he said were sacred, a dance he did bowing and praying. He mentioned some spirits, names I never heard and sure as hell can't spell. Guess he likes being in that cabin because maybe alone he can believe he still has a place for himself, and now for his Indian kid, even if they are alone in a small cabin up on that huge, wild mountain. Maybe he feels protected there. I sure hope somebody or something somewhere is protecting him."

"William, that cabin and that mountain and those spirits he talks of may be all he really has," Talbot stated. "I can make him a deputy for a while, give him something in town, maybe he and Courtney can find some place for themselves here. I'm willing to try to help him. Last year he saved my life twice, once here at Milly's and then at Reiser, and the least I can do now is return the favor as best I can."

"You know, Jim," replied Johnson, "that'd be really decent of you. Lord knows the man can handle a gun."

"Hell, two guns!" Talbot replied. "Fastest damn gun I've ever seen."

"Well gentlemen," Swanson said as he stood up, "on that note, if you'll pardon me I must see about Miss Roxy. We' agreed to meet once I returned from hunting with Johnny. Thanks for the company. Dr. Mark Johnson, sure is a great pleasure seeing you again. Hope I'll see you two again soon. And let's all hope for the best for our mutual friend Johnny Redfeather."

Swanson shook hands with Johnson and Talbot, then turned to Talbot. "Jim, we never did get back to talking about Bulger's invitation to go hunting. Perhaps we can do that some time soon. He asked me to ride out to his bunkhouse so we can set a date. Think I'll do that in the next few days, then visit you in your office afterwards."

"Good idea," Talbot replied. "Certainly before you go hunting with him. Come find me next week."

"I shall. Now if you'll excuse me. Oh, and I'll pay our bill here. My turn. I'll give Roxy the money."

"Well thank you, Bill" Talbot replied. "I was about to do that, but we sure appreciate your generosity. Enjoy Roxy's company, and maybe ask her to tell Marilee I'll look for her later. I should walk around a bit. Milly always likes me to make my presence known, especially on Saturday nights."

"I'll do that for sure, Jim" Swanson replied.

"Thank you kindly, William," Johnson said as Swanson turned to leave.

"My pleasure," Swanson added as he smiled over his shoulder and walked away. "Jim," Johnson said, "think I'll head out, get back to my cabin before night fall. Enjoyed the whiskey and the food, and, of course, the company. Good to be back in town. Bill Swanson sure is generous, isn't he?"

"He is indeed. Well, enjoy the rest of the evening Doc. Looks like a real pretty sunset coming on with those high clouds. Abigail and I used to love to sit on our porch and watch the summer sunsets over the mountains. Real nice that always was."

"Well, yes, a fine memory. Still so sorry for your loss. Well, say hello to Marilee for me. Tell her the steaks were fine. Maybe Sam has learned something about cooking meat while I was away."

"Well, maybe miracles, like Reverend Simpson is always saying, really do happen."

"Yeah," Johnson laughed, "maybe they do."

He smiled, shook Talbot's hand, then stood and walked out of the saloon, knowing how painfully inadequate his response to Talbot's memory of Abigail had been. Talbot collected the plates and carried them to the bar before starting his slow walk among Milly's patrons on yet another Saturday night in this tiny oasis in a vast, unforgiving wilderness.

18
Sheriff Talbot's Office

"Bill, good to see you here. Have a seat. Coffee?"

"Well, that's kind of you, Jim. I believe I will."

"Can't guarantee how good it might be. My wife Abigail used to make much better coffee than I ever hope to. Hope it doesn't prove fatal."

"Well, considering that I just missed getting bitten by a huge rattlesnake out at Smith's bunkhouse yesterday, I'm sure willing to take a chance on your coffee."

Swanson sat down on a rickety chair as Talbot brought two full cups to their table. "Might want to sip this a bit before you gulp it down. Just in case it really is dangerous to your health."

Swanson took two sips, then set the cup on the table. "Yeah, uh, that's strong all right. Might want to use a little less next time, maybe not bring it to a boil. Just get it warm."

"Yeah, that's good advice. I'll work on that. So, I take it you've been to Jesse Smith's place? You told me Saturday you would head out there later this week."

"Yes, right. Rode out there yesterday. Place was nearly deserted. Just Bulger and one or two others. Guess most of the men were out with the herds. Bulger and I agreed to go out next Sunday. Probably spend three or four days camped out somewhere, maybe a few more. We don't really have a definite plan. But you said last Saturday night at Milly's that we should talk about my going out with him."

"Yes. It's just because he lied to me about when he came to work for Smith. A man who lies about where he's been this close to the end of that war could have something to hide. And the way he just introduced himself back in Milly's that night. Almost like he knew who you were. But if so, how? From where?"

"Well, I did escape that prison with Johnny Redfeather, and you're right that both sides wanted his scalp by the end of the war. But I just don't see a connection between any of that and Bulger," Swanson said as he took a big gulp of his coffee. "Whew! Yeah, strong."

"I don't either, at least not now," Talbot said as he drank again. "But I'd say again just be really careful when you're out with him. Watch your back. Maybe you can find out more about him without saying too much. Want more coffee?"

"Ah, no, thank you. This is fine. Well, okay, I'll watch my back, as you say, and also what I say. I'll come visit again after I return."

"Good. I'll look forward to seeing you then. Any idea where you two will be headed?"

"No, not yet. Hunting was really good with Johnny up in Raven Meadow. But his cabin is way up on that big mountain, and I sure don't want Bulger, or anybody else for that matter, learning that. The trail to Johnny's cabin is on the far eastern edge of the meadow, and it's not easy to find. I could lead Bulger to that meadow without letting on where that trail is. That would definitely feel like a betrayal of Johnny."

"Yes, it would, and neither of us wants that," Talbot added.

Swanson stood, and shook Talbot's hand. "Thanks again, Jim. I am just so damn glad that I have met you again, especially way out here where I didn't expect to know anyone. Been a real pleasure, I must say. I'll be off now, and see about gear and ammunition. My blanket is worn too thin to keep a squirrel warm. Time for a new one. I'll see you probably sometime late next week. Oh, and thanks for the coffee."

"Sure thing, Bill. See you back here in a week or so."

19
Green River Town

On Saturday June 15 the sun exploded from behind the mountains east of Green River into a perfectly clear morning. A slight breeze swayed leaves on deciduous trees, orchestrating rhythmic dances on the walls of buildings. Light streaked across the river's surface, illuminating the spray cast aloft as water churned around boulders and downed trees.

By nine o'clock most of the businesses on both sides of what passed for Main Street were busy serving the usual mix of customers in a frontier town. Shop owners between the stage coach station at the southern end of the boardwalk, and the last crumbling planks at Hal's saloon on the northern end, eagerly opened their doors. Josh Brown, the proprietor of Green River Grocery, and his clerks were stacking dry goods that had arrived the night before. Justin Cranker and his son Aaron were slicing and packaging beef slaughtered on Friday at the stockyards outside town for the evening meals at Green River's saloons and restaurants. At the men's and women's haberdasher shops across the dusty street from Milly's Saloon, owner Julie Emerson arranged the "latest fashions" from, she claimed on signs taped to her shop windows, the "finest European cloth makers," plus "handmade jewelry" straight from "Kansas City and other big eastern cities."

Across from Hal's Saloon Bill Haggerty, owner of Haggerty's Blacksmith Shop, which a sign claimed was "the Finest in the West," struggled to weld the broken axles of two buggies that had collided Thursday night near the round-about. Brothers Bill and Jerome Burrows, owners of the town's feed store and nursery, just down the street from the bank, served several customers looking for vegetable seeds for summer gardens and bales of hay for their horses and livestock. At Dakota Outfitters men debated the cost of renting pack horses and outdoor equipment, including tents and cooking equipment, for extensive hunting trips into the mountains north and east of town. The Green River

Cafe served cups of steaming coffee and fresh rolls from Sara Jensen's New Dakota Bakery next door. The adjacent General Store, recently reopened by Jesse Wilkins after a fire in late March, was already crowded with men and women purchasing a large array of products, everything from household goods, pots and pans, gardening tools, hammers and nails, axes and shovels for small building and repair projects, cups, saucers, glasses and cloth table coverings to miners' picks, harnesses and saddles for herders, and hunting rifles. While their parents pondered their purchases and discussed prices with store clerks, small children outside kicked rubber balls back and forth, often dodging two-horse buggies barreling down the busy street.

In his little office Bartholomew Aloysius Simpson, the pastor of Green River Presbyterian Church who firmly believed in the spiritual symbolism and efficacy of his three names, searched both the Old and the New Testament for just the right message for tomorrow's sermon, which he had decided ought to be about justice being the Lord's, not man's. Later that afternoon he would lead the women's chorus, the "Army of the Righteous" as he liked to call them, in rehearsal for their singing at the ten o'clock service. Having decided against any further frontal assaults on Milly's Saloon, he still believed that eventually she and her husband Frank would come to a riveting service some fateful Sunday and be so overwhelmed by the power and truthfulness of his preaching that they would close their fiendish establishment the very next day. If he could close Milly's, Reverend Simpson believed, he could close all such satanic establishments in Green River and eventually become the spiritual savior of the entire Dakota Territory.

Inside their saloon Milly and Frank, helped by Sam and Amanda, as she was now called, began cleaning up tables from an exceptionally busy Friday night. Owing to a rowdy drinking contest involving several railroad workers that had started just before midnight, beer and whiskey glasses remained on several tables, and several broken glasses littered the floor. When Amanda opened the front doors to sweep out the floor, she encountered a man lying face down on the boardwalk. She whacked his head with her broom, shouted "Git on outta my way," and rolled him into the street, only to discover a two-inch gash in his forehead. Back inside, she shouted, "Sam, get me a bucket of water. Got a drunk here needs tending to."

"Sure enough," Sam agreed, and returned a moment later with a bucked of soapy dish water.

"Here you go," he said. "This will wake up a dead man, maybe two," and walked back toward the kitchen behind the bar. Amanda dumped the entire bucket-full on the man's head. Startled awake, the man rolled over, shouted "You lousy little tramp, I'll show you," and was about to draw his gun when Johnny Redfeather suddenly appeared in the doorway with both guns drawn. "Now what was that you said to my lieutenant, mister?" Johnny asked calmly. "You aren't gonna be showing anybody anything. Put that gun down and get away from here. Now!" Johnny yelled, and aimed a pistol at the man's head. "And I don't think you want to be coming back here anytime soon. Now git!" The man picked up his hat and stumbled up the boardwalk toward Hal's Saloon.

"Lieutenant," Johnny added, "next time you figure on throwing a bucket of water at a man dead drunk, call me first. No telling what a man who is that bad drunk will do when he wakes up."

"Yes, sir," Amanda responded. "How'd you know what I was up to?"

"Oh, I heard Sam ask Milly for a bucket of water, and I figured after last night's whiskey battle in here there just might be a few left over that didn't quite quit the premises. Grogan pushed a few out the door, and I shoved one back out when he tried to come back in again. Figured one or two of them could not walk more than a few steps, so might be spending the night outside on the boards. Nasty when they wake up! Now, let's go get breakfast. Mama's awful hungry upstairs, and she's sent me down for some coffee and grub. Sure don't want to get her screaming at me or anyone else this hour of the morning."

"I reckon. Thank you, Johnny."

"You're welcome! Now let's see what Sam's cooking."

§

Around eleven o'clock Jim Talbot halted his buggy at the roundabout in the center of town. He had sat on its circular bench for several minutes the night of the raid on Milly's Saloon, when he first realized how volatile Green River and its environs had become and how dangerous his position as sheriff was.

"Whatever we stopping here for, Jim?" Marilee asked. "I really should get back to Milly's."

"Oh, I like this spot. I pass it every day walking around town and back to my office. I always think of Johnny when I'm here, almost like he and I are the Indian and the white man of the statue clasping each other's forearm in that gesture of, I guess, brotherhood. Nice ideal. Don't know what chance it has in reality anymore. You say to me 'There's always duty,' and you're right, Marilee. I'm right in the middle of whatever is left after Reiser Canyon, and you will just have to accept that. I'm not leaving my responsibility as sheriff, not after Abigail's horrible death. That would be a betrayal, as if I could just walk away from bringing her out here just to have some lousy drunk send a bullet into her beautiful face."

"Jim, I will never ask you to forget Abigail, or to leave being sheriff. I know better than that, honest. I am just trying to think about a life for us, that's all. For now, thank you for our few nights and mornings together. It's real pretty at your cabin. Peaceful. Maybe more nights and mornings together will be good for both of us."

"Yes. I'm sure you are right. For now, we both better get on back." He leaned over and kissed Marilee, who accepted his lips warmly. Then he sat up and whipped the reins. "Git on up, now," he called as the buggy hurried down the dusty way toward Milly's.

20
Hunter and Hunted

In front of the Dakota Hotel around 12:30 the following Sunday afternoon, Swanson and Bulger checked their gear and ammunition. "Bedroll, lean-to, canteen, blankets, few pots, food, rifles and ammunition. Guess we got everything we'll need for a few days and nights," Bulger said. "You got any preference for where we go?"

"Well, not really. Last week I hunted with Johnny Redfeather up in Raven Meadow. Got us a deer and an elk pretty quickly. But I am sure there are other places we could go. This is real big country with lots of game. Any other suggestions?"

"Well, we could head up to Reiser Canyon, but I gather that's where that attack on the Cheyenne happened a while back. Not too sure who's still up in that area, and maybe that's bad luck, seeing as how I heard a hell of a lot of blood was shed there. Eagle Canyon has lots of elk, but it's supposed to be sacred to the Indians, so best to just leave it alone now. Maybe somewhere around Raven Meadow then, like you suggested, would be better."

Remembering his conversation with Sheriff Talbot four days earlier, Swanson hesitated, suddenly wishing he had not even mentioned Raven Meadow. However, after several seconds he convinced himself that he was right about the isolated location of the trail up the mountain to Redfeather's cabin.

"Sure, all right," Swanson said finally, "let's head to Raven Meadow. It's due east, and we can get to the meadow in less than two hours of good riding. Let's load up and head out."

Bulger turned toward his horse and loaded two heavily laden saddle bags. He then mounted, and checked the holster on his right hip for his Remington 44. As Swanson mounted his horse, Bulger noticed that he was not carrying a pistol.

After riding for just over two hours, Bulger and Swanson halted. Before them stretched the expansive beauty of Raven Meadow, dotted by emerging shoots of paintbrush, glacier lilies, and a few bluebells poking above the remaining layer of snow. "Beautiful place," Swanson remarked, enjoying not only his view but also the memory of his days here with Johnny Redfeather.

"Yeah, guess you could say that," Bulger replied, "but I'm just thinking of hunting right now. We need to find some water, and a good place to camp, then start looking for some game. Whereabouts did you and Redfeather camp?"

Swanson hesitated, remembering that the clump of trees from where Johnny had shot the deer their first night was due east, close to the obscure trail to his cabin, and that he had promised Sheriff Talbot he would not betray Johnny's sanctuary. "Well," Swanson began, "not quite sure now. Whole meadow looks the same. Think we rode straight from here toward the middle. We weren't too close to the mountain, that I'm sure of."

"Okay, whatever you say. Lead on," Bulger agreed, and followed closely behind. Swanson guided his horse north toward a cluster of boulders and pine trees that he could see about two hundred yards ahead. When they reached the boulders, Swanson dismounted, removed his saddlebags and laid them down, tethered his horse to a large tree, and turned toward Bulger.

"This spot should work well," Swanson said. "The boulders will shelter us from the wind tonight, and we might hang our food in one of those trees. This look okay for you?"

"Sure, why not? Good as any I figure," Bulger agreed. He dismounted, tethered his horse next to Swanson's, and removed his saddlebags. Swanson untied his and began setting out the cooking utensils and his bedroll, then stuffed their food in a sack and suspended it from one of the higher branches of a tree some thirty yards away. One hour later they had set up camp for the night, and both men propped their rifles against the boulders. Bulger noticed again that Swanson did not have a pistol among his gear, though he did have two hunting rifles.

"So, time to go see what we can find, Colonel?" Bulger asked as he checked that his rifle was loaded. "Sounds fine," Swanson added, and they began walking further north into the meadow. "I think Johnny and I bagged our deer just a few hundred yards ahead, near another clump of trees. We can try using that area first, sort of a blind."

"That sounds like a good idea," Bulger replied. "No sense giving ourselves away if we don't have to."

Each carried his rifle and a box of ammunition, and Bulger also carried his pistol. After walking for about twenty minutes, Swanson asked, "Say Jake, I noticed back at the hotel that you were carrying a pistol. Mind if I ask what you mean to do with that on a hunting trip?"

"Well, you might say I've gotten used to carrying it. Sure a rifle is a better bet for hunting, but just the same, I might need it. Never know out here."

They approached the trees and laid their rifles against the trunk of a large cottonwood. Bulger adjusted the holster on his hip, then turned to Swanson. "We're after deer, right, for the first day? Just get us something we can slice up and cook tonight. Maybe tomorrow hope to bag an elk with a large rack, a trophy we can take back to town. That about how you figured it?",

"Sure, fine," Swanson responded, glancing again at the pistol on Bulger's hip. "Whoever gets the first sighting gets the first shot. That's how Johnny and I proceeded. Seems fair to me."

"Fine idea, Colonel. I'll go for that."

Each moved to one side of a huge boulder and leaned against it. Swanson wondered again why Bulger was carrying a Remington 44. As it was a common weapon in the war, Swanson realized that he could not know on which side Bulger had fought. He realized that Bulger's lie about when he started herding for Tompkin did not mean that he had not been a soldier at some time in the war. Still, as he and Redfeather had agreed, "liars are scum," and Swanson knew that he had better be careful.

After forty minutes, Bulger said suddenly, "Colonel, here comes our dinner!" Swanson looked up to see several deer headed toward them only fifty yards away, stopping occasionally to eat vegetation they uncovered in the snow. "Yeah," Swanson said, "I see them. First shot is yours."

As the deer approached within twenty yards, Bulger lowed his rifle and fired. A small doe fell immediately. "Fine shot," Swanson cried. As the other animals scattered wildly, the men emerged from behind the boulder and walked to the fallen animal. Bulger had shot it right between its eyes. "At that distance that's impressive shooting," Swanson proclaimed. "Where'd you learn to shoot that well?"

"Practice. Lots of it."

"In the war?" Swanson asked.

"In and out, you might say," Bulger responded. "Now let's get our supper back to camp, gut it and get it on a fire. I'm getting hungry."

Several hours later Bulger had finished skinning and carving the deer. Swanson laid the cuts of meat on a grill placed over two rocks, lighted twigs and wood underneath, then took tin plates and utensils out of his saddlebags and laid them on a wool blanket he had spread between them.

"Done a lot of cooking?" Bulger asked as he watched Swanson turning over the slabs of meat on the grill.

"Yeah, did my share in the war. We had cooks, of course, but sometimes I volunteered to help with the meals. Just to show my men how much I cared for them. You know, try to be one of them. Officers usually got much better food than the enlisted soldiers, so I thought if I could help prepare some of their meals I might garner some good will, maybe even some respect among them."

"Well, that's a fine idea. I take it you were Union, right? You don't sound Southern."

"Yeah, that's right. Maine actually. Got a commission at West Point, served three years all told, but last two years mostly in the South. Georgia, Tennessee."

"Georgia? Whereabouts?"

Remembering Sheriff Talbot's warning about revealing too much of himself to a known liar, Swanson hesitated. He focused on the deer meat cooking slowly on the grill, and reached for some more wood and placed it under the grill.

"Oh, mostly northwest near Tennessee, then across Georgia to near South Carolina. Bunch of battles I'd prefer to forget. Hell of a lot of killing the last two years. Why do you ask? Were you Rebel?"

"Yeah, Rebel. Lots of time in Georgia, mostly east, like you say, near South Carolina. You ever captured?"

Swanson paused and glanced quickly toward the fire. "Me? No. I knew men who were though. Terrible torture inflicted on some of them. Just barbaric. Maybe worse than the actual fighting. What about you?"

"Never captured, but like you I later knew men who were. Guess most prisoner camps were just awful. My brother Hank worked for a few months at Camp Lawton Prison in Georgia. He told me that wasn't so bad a place, compared to some of the others. Andersonville, I guess, was brutal."

At Bulger's sudden mention of Lawton, Swanson stiffened. "So I heard. Hundreds died there, starvation, sickness, god-damn lice everywhere. Men just eaten alive." Swanson turned his back on Bulger and toward the fire. "Speaking of eating, I'd better check our dinner." He stirred the wood under the grill, then again flipped the meat. As he did so, he realized that one of the men Redfeather had killed when they escaped could well have been Bulger's brother.

"I heard Lawton was closed in November sixty-four," Swanson said as he turned back toward Bulger. "Sherman was coming fast, and the Union soldiers burned what was left of it. Was your brother still there when the Union came through?"

"No, Hank died shortly before Sherman arrived. He was just a kid, really."

"I see," Swanson replied cautiously. "Sure sorry to hear that."

"Yeah, I was furious when I heard he had been killed. You lose anybody in the war?"

"Well, no relatives, if that's what you mean. Had no brothers or sisters. Folks died after the war ended. Lost many friends though. Everybody lost friends. Say, let's eat. Meat looks just about right. I brought some bread too. If you'll cut the meat into smaller pieces, I'll cut the bread."

"Sounds good. Thanks for cooking. The meat looks darn tasty."

"You're welcome."

Bulger placed several cuts of meat on a plate and handed it to Swanson before settling his own plate on his knees. "That's about an even split. Let me know if you want more."

"Sure, thanks," Swanson added. The men ate in silence, each trying to imagine what the other was thinking. After finishing his meal, Bulger asked, "Colonel, you want some whiskey to wash all that down? I've got a bottle in my saddlebag."

"Well, yes. Thanks," Swanson replied. "Want me to go get it for you?"

"No, I'll get it. I know right where it is," Bulger said as he rose and walked to his horse. He returned five minutes later with a bottle and two small tin cups.

"Have a shot, Colonel. Might as well enjoy it, even out here. Never know when it could be your last. Anyone who's been in war knows that truth." They clinked their cups and drank.

"You're speaking truth there, Jake. I swear half the times I bed down in some field somewhere in Georgia I was sure I would never see another sunrise. Terrible way to live, if being in war can even be called living."

"Doubt it. I think of my brother Hank often, how the war took him so young. He never got to know living past the war."

"Know how he died?"

"Not sure, really. Have to assume it was in battle. Never did find out. Won't ever know now."

"Suppose not. Too late. Mad dogs and coyotes ate whatever might have been left out on a battlefield. Very sorry, Jake."

"Yeah, just a kid."

Sensing the rising anxiety in Bulger's voice, Swanson reached across the blanket for his plate. "Think I'll wash these plates in that stream we passed riding in. I'll leave the cups, in case we both want more whiskey." He rose and carried the plates to a stream about sixty yards away. As he rinsed the plates, he sensed the increasing anger in Bulger's voice and its potential danger. For the first time since they had left Green River he regretted not having carried a pistol. The man whose throat Redfeather had slit and left to die on the prison floor was young, but Swanson had no way of knowing if that was Bulger's brother or if he was honest about assuming his brother had died in battle. "The old hatreds," he thought. "Just never die." He realized that he could not easily conceal one of his hunting rifles near his bedroll, and that doing so would immediately signal his fear of Bulger. He did not want to risk escalating the tension that had suddenly developed between them, and he resolved to be as cautious as possible.

Back at their campsite, Swanson returned the plates to his saddlebags, then sat down across the fire from Bulger. "Jake, how about another whiskey before we turn in for the night?"

"Thought you'd never ask," Bulger laughed, and poured generous shots into both cups. "This might take the chill out of the air. Nights still cold up high."

"That they are," Swanson agreed, and downed his whiskey. "Think I'll drag what's left of this deer away from here, maybe to that stream, and string up the rest of our food, then maybe go for a little walk."

"Okay. I'll feed the horses and set out the bedrolls and find a tree limb and some rocks for the tarp. Have it all ready by the time you get back."

"Thanks, see you a bit later." Swanson swung a saddlebag and some rope over his shoulder, then began dragging the carcass across the meadow to a clump of oak trees down from a bend in the stream. "Mostly bone," he mused, "coyotes can chew on it all night." He walked back to the bend where the stream, fed now by snow melt from Raven Mountain's glaciers, churned over rocks as it carved an ever-widening channel. Bulger's statement that his brother had died young gnawed on Swanson's conscience. "Many young men died in prisons," he told himself, "whether from torture, beatings, shooting, lice. Or slit throats." As the face of the young soldier gripping his gushing throat flashed in his memory, Swanson stuck this hand into the stream. "Yes," he thought, "this will do." He stripped naked and waded in, cupping cold water in his hands and splashing it all over his dusty, tired body. He shivered as the chilling water cascaded over his shoulders and down his torso to his genitals and legs. He stood for a moment in the stream now swirling over his calves, shivering in the night air but also feeling cleansed by the careening water. "For that boy, whoever he was," Swanson said aloud, "For that boy. It was war. Johnny knew war. Johnny knew what was about to happen to some of my men. He knew!" And cupping his hands he poured generous amounts of water over his head until his whole body shook.

Moments later he stepped out of the stream and reached for his clothes. He used his shirt to wipe himself down, then dressed, hoping his body warmth would eventually dry his clothes before he crawled into his bedroll. "I must walk, try to warm up," he thought. He began walking east toward the base of Raven Mountain. After several minutes, he stopped and looked up. Orion glowed in the early summer sky. "Hunter," Swanson thought. "Who is the hunter, who the hunted?" He stood still for several moments, still shivering, but transfixed by the huge constellation that dominated the vast panorama above him. "What care any of Johnny Redfeather's gods, or mine, for him or me in this wilderness? Nothing!" he concluded, and began walking back toward camp.

When he arrived, Bulger was waiting for him. "Wanted to make sure you didn't get lost, or eaten by some hungry bear or mountain lion. Lots of both out here."

"Yeah, true enough. Johnny warned me about that the night we camped in this meadow. Can't be too careful I guess."

"Right. Why I brought the pistol that you asked me about earlier. Lot handier than a rifle in a surprise attack. I'll keep it near my bedroll. Think I'll turn in. Been a long day, and night's getting down right cold."

"Agreed. I stashed the carcass and strung up the rest of the food. Should be all right tonight."

"Good. Thanks. See you tomorrow."

Swanson, still shivering in his damp clothes, eagerly crawled into his bed-roll under the tarp and pulled a heavy wool blanket over him. The last, faint light of day lingered precariously on the western wall of Raven Mountain, then suddenly disappeared. Above him a trillion stars filled the heavens with fantastical shapes. Amid the sounds of crickets and the scuttling of small animals near their fire pit, Swanson contemplated the immense silence of the light show blazing above him. Although sleep summoned, his restless mind churned. Was there any possible connection between Hank Bulger and his and Redfeather's escape from Lawton Prison? Could he have been...?"

Unable to resist any longer, Swanson succumbed to a sleep deeper than the deepest canyons on Raven Mountain.

§

Bulger awoke just as the sunlight slipped over the rim of Raven Mountain. Several inches of fresh snow blanketed the meadow. "Goddamnit! Snow! Not what I need. Shit!" he thought as he slid out of his bedroll. Seeing that Swanson was still asleep, Bulger stuck his revolver into his belt and covered the handle with his leather vest. He gathered whatever dry twigs he could find under the snow-cover, picked some moss from several pine trees, placed it all under the grill, then struck a match. Once the fire was rekindled he walked to the bend in the stream, retrieved the food sack Swanson had hung there, and filled a battered pot with water. Noticing tracks along the side of the stream, he followed them around the bend and saw that the carcass of the doe had been picked clean by the night's hungry scavengers.

Back at the fire he stuck more kindling under the grill, then put the pot for coffee and several slabs of bacon on the grill. He sat still, eyeing Swanson still slumbering under the tarp. After several minutes, Bulger called to him, "Hey, Colonel, time to get up. Coffee and bacon 'bout ready."

Swanson rolled over and faced Bulger. "Whoa, didn't mean to sleep so long. Thanks for getting up breakfast. Food all right?"

"Food was fine. Let's eat. Sun's coming up and I figure we should go back to those boulders and start looking for more game. Think today I'd like to bag an elk. That sound all right with you?"

"Yeah, sure. Soon as I wake up, get out of this bedroll and get some of that coffee and bacon I'm smelling, I'll be ready to go."

Swanson stood up, stretched, and reached for his boots. Bulger took his gun out of his belt. "Never mind the boots, Colonel, you won't be needing them."

"What?" Swanson gasped, as Bulger pointed his pistol at Swanson's head. "What the hell is this about, Jake?"

"You know god-damn well what this is about, Swanson, you stinking Yankee! Don't pretend! It's about Lawton Prison and my brother, Hank. You and that lousy redskin slit his throat when you escaped and left him on the dirt floor to bleed to death. Don't ask me what this is about!"

Swanson stepped back, holding his hands out in front of him. "So, that kid was your brother. Look, Jake, you and I both know what those crazed guards were about to do to my men. Don't tell me you don't know that. We could not allow that to happen. No decent man would. It was war, sure, but god-damnit, shoving a hot poker into a defenseless prisoner is just barbarism, hardly a fair battle. And Johnny and I could not tolerate that. You wouldn't either."

"Yeah, well, maybe I would and maybe I wouldn't. But what I won't tolerate is some bastard traitor slitting Hank's throat like he's some sort of wild animal, then just leavin' him bleeding. Just like what I saw Redfeather do to Tompkin up in Reiser Canyon."

"Reiser? So you lied when you told the sheriff you weren't at that raid! Tompkin's barbarians slaughtered women and children!"

"Yeah, so what? Who cares about a bunch of red savages?"

"Savages! Who's calling Indians savages after that raid?"

"They got what they deserved. Tompkin told me that a bunch of them, Apache he thinks, killed his parents right in front of him years ago, when he was just a kid. He's right! There's no room for any of them out here, don't matter what tribe."

"Listen, Jake, you're mad with revenge. Crazy! There's no point in that any more. The war is over, and the past can't be fixed. For Christ's sake, just put that gun down and listen to me."

"I'm through listening to you, Swanson! Unless, that is, you decide to tell me where Redfeather's cabin is. He's the one I really want. I heard you and Talbot talking at Milly's a while back about Redfeather having a cabin in these mountains somewhere, and I want you to tell me where it is. Now! Or else!"

"Or else? Ha! You'll shoot me even if I do tell you. You think I'm that stupid?"

"Swanson, just tell me! Or tell me where you want the first bullet, cause there's gonna be a few. You're gonna die just like Hank did. Slowly, painfully, watching your blood drip onto the pretty white snow. Tell me, god-damnit!"

Swanson straightened his back and put his hands on his hips. "No. I won't tell you that. I will not betray Johnny Redfeather. Not after he saved me and my men at Lawton. Never! Jake, the war is over. Nothing about that can be changed or fixed. It's too late for that. I...."

Bulger shot Swanson in both his knees, then laughed as he screamed and crumbled backward. "There, you lousy Union bastard, down where you belong. In the bloody dirt. Just like Hank." Bulger fired again into Swanson's left shoulder. "No, no!" Swanson screamed in agony as he rolled over. "There, that ought to do it. I'll just sit here and eat some bacon, have some coffee, then pack up this little camp while you bleed to death. Any questions you want to ask before I leave?"

"Jake, killing me this way will solve nothing," Swanson gasped as he clawed the snow with his right hand.

"The hell it won't! I'll get Redfeather one way or another, and then my brother's ghost will stop following me, begging to know when I'm gonna finally avenge his death. Won't be long now. So long—Colonel! Ha!"

Bulger sat on the ground in front of the fire and slowly ate the bacon, then drank a cup of coffee, all the while relishing Swanson's groans and watching the streams of blood flowing from his wounds. He then dismantled the lean-to and loaded it and his bedroll onto his horse. "Hey, Colonel," he shouted, "I'll leave you your bedroll in case you want a warm place to die later this morning. Ain't that nice of me?" Laughing loudly, Bulger stuffed the tin plates and utensils into a saddlebag, along with the remaining food. "No sense leavin' all this food for the scavengers," he decided. "They'll smell the blood and feast on what's left of him. Time to get out of here." He tucked his rifle into his saddle, then noticed both of Swanson's still leaning against a boulder. "Shit! Why not? Swanson won't be needing a gun any more. Why waste a fine rifle on a dead man?" He grabbed one of Swanson's rifles, mounted his horse, then turned toward Swanson, moaning and sprawled beneath him in a growing pool of blood. "You bastard, Bulger, you bastard," Swanson screamed as Bulger aimed his own rifle at his head. "Nah," he yelled, "I'll just let you bleed to death. Just like Hank." He fired into Swanson's left thigh, then turned his horse and, carrying Swanson's rifle in his right hand, began riding toward the forest.

"Johnny, Johnny! Message," Swanson groaned as he agonizingly heaved his body over his left side and lay face down in the snow. Using only his right forearm he slowly, painfully pulled his body forward and as far under the shade of a large pine tree as he could. Near the trunk, in snow he was sure would not soon melt, he scrawled "bulger lawton" in crooked letters with his index finger. "Johnny, Johnny," he muttered, "I did not betray you. I did not." Minutes later he died.

§

As he neared the forest, Bulger glimpsed a large shadowy creature moving slowly through the thick undergrowth near a grove of white pines. He slowed his horse and, when the creature stopped, he halted. Although he initially believed that it was moving upright, he quickly dismissed that possibility. "Must be a huge, god-damn grizzly rearing on its hind feet," he reflected. "Only thing that big out here." He reached for his rifle, and was about to dismount when the creature resumed moving slowly to his right. Although its form remained indistinct among the dense stands of pine and cottonwoods, when Bulger again saw it for a split-second through the heavy underbrush it still seemed to be moving upright. "Oh for Christ's sake," he muttered, "is this Swanson's big god-damn ghost walking through the woods, coming after me already? What am I, nuts? It's a grizzly!" Not wanting to risk wounding and thus enraging the dangerous animal, Bulger held his fire and for several minutes sat still in his saddle. Unable to discern whatever was there, yet aware that he now had to reach the herders' bunkhouse quickly, he finally decided that he could not linger. Holding the reins with his left hand and the rifle with his right, he cautiously urged his horse deeper into the forest, convinced that the rustling branches and crunching sound meant that the creature was moving slowly away from him.

When the sounds suddenly ceased, Bulger halted, fearing an immediate attack. For several seconds neither he nor the creature moved. When the sounds resumed, Bulger exhaled deeply, then resumed riding slowly forward, believing that the creature was again moving away from him. But twice during the next several minutes his horse, whinnying frantically, suddenly halted, reared, and the second time nearly threw Bulger to the ground. Desperately trying to control the animal, Bulger pulled as hard as he could on the reins with both hands. In has panic he dropped Swanson's rifle and, too frightened to retrieve it, whipped the horse furiously and did not stop until he had left the forest completely.

Hestovatohkeo'o moved to a clearing. One face looked toward the meadow where Swanson's body lay in the snow, the other toward Bulger's horse galloping madly away.

21
Jake Bulger's Retreat

Five hours later Jake Bulger arrived at Jesse Smith's bunkhouse, dismounted, and knocked on the door. "Well, didn't expect to see you for another two or three days at least," Smith said as he opened the door. "Thought you were headed for a longer hunting trip."

"Well, Swanson and I got us a deer yesterday, then this morning he wasn't feeling too good, so we decided to head back. Don't know quite what's wrong with him, but he figured it wasn't too good an idea to stay out there any longer. He's back in town I'd guess. Say, Jesse, I've decided I'd like to move on. Getting tired of herding, want to try something else for a while. Mind if I collect my pay now? I'd sure appreciate that."

"Well, all right. Once we had our little talk you've been good with the herd. Wait here. I'll be right back."

Fifteen minutes later Smith returned and handed Bulger a roll of bills. "That should about cover it. Good luck. Maybe see you around here later on. Where you headed, just in case someone comes asking about you?"

"Don't know for sure. Maybe back down south to Texas. Maybe back to Denver. Not quite sure at the moment. Just whatever suits me, I guess."

"I see. Well, safe riding wherever you go. Good luck."

"Thanks, Jesse. Good luck to you and the men."

Bulger shook Smith's hand, then mounted and directed his horse to a trail that swung south-west and crossed the river about four miles south of town. Once across the rickety wooden bridge, which he noticed was missing several planks, Bulger rode until he came to the sprawling Union Pacific railroad site. He approached the bunkhouse and canteen behind a pile of discarded steel rails and wooden ties scattered across the desert landscape, the detritus of mechanized westward expansion encroaching on Green River. He dismounted, tethered his horse to a lonely tree near the bunkhouse, and rapped on the front door. A large brown-skinned man, reeking of alcohol, opened the door.

"Yeah, whattta you want?"

"I'm lookin' for Jeb Carlson. Is he here?"

"No, Jeb ain't here. Why? Who's lookin' for him?"

"Name's Jake Bulger. Friend of his from some time back. He comin' back tonight?"

"No, not till tomorrow. Why?"

"I was wondering if I could bunk here tonight. I'm thinkin' about trying to get on with the railroad."

"Nah, no strangers in here. Got to wait till Jeb returns. You can bunk only if he says so. Jeb don't cotton to nobody he doesn't know. There's some trees left out back closer to the river. You can camp there tonight, see about Jeb tomorrow."

"I see. Well, all right. Guess that will have to do. What time you figurin' Jeb to return?"

"Ain't figurin' nothin'. He's out huntin' savages again along the train route. He just comes back when he's done for the day. No telling when really. Just come back late tomorrow. Should be here, just not sure exactly when is all."

"I see. All right, I'll see you tomorrow."

"Guess so," the man said as he slammed the door shut.

§

Jeb Carlson returned to the Union Pacific bunkhouse at two o'clock the next day. "Hey Jeb," said Josh Marquez, the man who had greeted Bulger the day before, "a guy named Bulger was here yesterday askin' about bunkin' here. Said he knew you from a ways back. I told him not till you returned. Think he camped out by the trees near the river."

"Bulger? Jake Bulger? What the hell is he doing here?"

"Don't know, he just said he knew you. Somethin' about working on the railroad. I told him you'd be here sometime today. Hasn't been back since."

"Well, I'll go look for him. See what he wants. Damn surprised to hear from him."

Jeb Carlson walked down a path toward a scattering of cottonwoods at the river's edge. He found Jake Bulger leaning against a tree.

"Jake, what are you doing here? Aren't you still riding with Smith's herders?"

"Ah, Jeb, glad you're back. No, I had a disagreement, shall we say, with one or two of Smith's men, so I decided to quit. Little issue of a poker game and lots of cash, so I decided to take my pay and leave. Told Smith I didn't like the idea of someone aiming a forty-four at my back just because of a lousy poker game. He said all right and gave me my pay. So here I am."

"Well, I haven't seen you for a while, nearly two months I think. You been in town at all?"

"No, not much. Been herding mostly. Say, any chance I could hold up here for a while, maybe do some work? I don't want to go near Smith's men again, not after our little poker disagreement. I got my back pay so I can pay for meals. Might not stay long, maybe go back to Denver pretty quick. Just not sure when right now."

"Sure, you can bunk here. We got room. I'll see about getting you some track work, maybe earn a few dollars more. Come on back with me. Meet some of the men, especially Marquez. He runs the bunkhouse, can show you where you can stash your stuff. Best stay on his right side. He took over from O'Sullivan. Just make sure you don't cross him, especially when he's drinking, which he does most of the time."

"I appreciate that. I'll stay clear of him as best I can."

"Good. Now let's go up there and get you settled."

22
Search Party

"He talked a lot about Raven Meadow is all I remember," Roxy told Talbot and Redfeather the following Thursday morning in Milly's. "That was seven, maybe eight days ago. Said he really enjoyed being with Johnny up in that meadow. That's all I know, Sheriff."

"Johnny, we need to get up there right away. No telling what's happened. If Bulger is still alive, he is probably back at Jesse Smith's bunkhouse, but if he is and he cared at all about Swanson he sure would have come to us. So I'm betting he doesn't care, or maybe at best just does not know. But even then, it seems he would have told us something by now."

"Sheriff," Johnny said, "I'll be all go to hell but this isn't good, no matter which way we cut it. That man lied about being with Tompkin in Reiser Canyon, and you and I both wish Swanson hadn't gone hunting with him. If we go up there, we go well armed. This situation stinks, and we aren't even there yet!"

"Right! How long will it take us to get to that meadow?"

"Hard ride, about two hours, maybe a bit less. We leave now, can be there by two o'clock I'd say."

"All right, I'll tell Butch he's in charge down here, and we'll leave right away. You lead, Johnny."

"Right, Sheriff."

§

After an hour's ride they began noticing the tracks of a single horse in the fresh snow heading out of the forest near less distinct tracks of two horses heading in. "Sheriff," Redfeather exclaimed, "only one man returned from that hunting trip, and it wasn't Colonel Swanson."

"Keep riding, Johnny. We don't know anything for sure yet."

Shortly thereafter Redfeather recognized the intricately carved, reddish stock of Swanson's rifle protruding from the snow in a grove of white pines. "Sheriff, that's Swanson's rifle," he yelled. "Fancy carved stock. Damnit! Where is he?"

"Johnny, you sure that's his?"

"Yes! Never seen a stock like that! And still only one set of tracks heading out. We have to get to that meadow. I'll pick up the rifle, take it with us."

"Right. Go!"

Redfeather followed the tracks of the single rider north into the meadow. Thirty minutes later he spotted the body lying half-buried in the snow. He galloped furiously toward it, then leapt from his horse and raced to Swanson's corpse. Blood from his eviscerated body pooled in the snow around which were tracks of numerous animals, including wolves and coyotes, that had fed upon the corpse every morning as the sun warmed the remains. Johnny screamed "No! No!" as he knelt and touched what was left of Swanson's right arm. "Colonel, this time you're not coming back from the dead like you did at Milly's. Even snakes in a god-damn swamp wouldn't do this. Not even your spirit can survive this." And he hurled a hideous howl to the sky that the winds carried around the mountains and across the meadow. But nothing answered.

Talbot dismounted and ran to Johnny, knelt behind him, and grabbed him firmly by the shoulders as he began retching. Talbot held Redfeather to his chest as he heaved. Johnny began wiping his hands over and over in the bloody snow, then, exhausted, fell back into Talbot's arms. They stayed in this position for several minutes, until Talbot looked up and to his right.

"Johnny, there's something scribbled in the snow, just above Swanson's right hand. Look!"

Redfeather looked up, then crawled toward the scratching in the snow. "Sheriff, two words: lawton and bulger. Oh hell! No! No! Sheriff, Lawton is that Georgia prison we escaped from. But why would Bulger want to kill Colonel? Makes no sense."

"Johnny, look where Swanson was shot. His thigh and shoulder, and the knees. Bulger wanted Swanson to die slowly, painfully. If Bulger had wanted to kill Swanson outright he would have shot him in the head.

But that's not what he did. Why? Maybe someone he knew at Lawton, maybe...."

"The kid! That kid whose throat I slit. He jumped me from behind and I drew my knife and cut his throat, then just left him cause we had to get out of there fast. God-damnit, I'll bet that was Bulger's kid brother! Colonel wanted to tell me. And that means Bulger's after me next, seeing as how I'm the one actually sliced that kid's neck. I'll be all go to hell if that's not the truth here. Colonel did nothing to deserve this." Johnny bent over, moaning, weeping, slowly repeating Colonel Swanson's name.

Talbot stood and moved to Redfeather, who remained crouched over, his clothes now soaked in bloody snow and dirt. Talbot knelt beside Redfeather and for a few minutes longer held his heaving shoulders. Then, content to allow him to experience his grief as he wished, Talbot rose and walked back to his horse, took a canteen out of his saddle bag, and walked to the stream. When he returned he offered the cold water to Redfeather, who drank heavily, then used the remains to wash his face and hands before rising to face Talbot.

"Sheriff, thank you. Sure am glad you are here. We got to bury what's left of Colonel Swanson up here, in this meadow."

"Sure, Johnny. Can't really move what's left of him. Lord knows there's been enough insult to his body already."

Redfeather stood and began mopping up the blood with dirt until it was nearly invisible, then scooped up batches of snow with which he wiped dried blood from what was left of Swanson's limbs and torso. He then removed his bandana from around his neck and walked to the stream, soaked it, and returned to Swanson's body and began gently wiping down the remains of Swanson's face and skull. When he had finished washing the remains he began piling rocks around the perimeter of the corpse, then filled in the spaces between the rocks with mud, grasses, some fireweed and paintbrush that grew nearby until he had covered Swanson's body completely. He returned to the stream, filled his hat with water, then returned and poured it slowly over the full length of the makeshift grave. He then knelt, bowed his head, and prayed softly. Talbot stood by silently, knowing that Johnny had to perform the burial ritual alone.

"Best we can do I figure, since we don't have a shovel," Redfeather said after several minutes. "Least ways now his spirit can wander, just like those Indian braves. Not all buried beneath the ground. Seek peace somewhere, like braves going to Seana, what you white folks call the Milky Way."

"Johnny, I'll gather some bigger rocks, make a marker of some kind. Seems we should do that."

"Yeah, okay, good idea." Together they gathered several larger rocks and laid them at the head of the burial mound. For several minutes Redfeather knelt on one knee near the marker. He then rose, turned to Talbot, and said quietly, "Time to go. Bulger is out there somewhere, and he wants to kill me. I got to get Amanda and Mama Dillard back up to my cabin first thing tomorrow. Someplace they can be safe. Maybe this mountain and Maheo can protect us. Guess I'll find out all right."

"Johnny, you know I will do all I can to protect you. We'll find Bulger before he can do any more harm. I promise you that."

"Sheriff, I do appreciate what you're saying, but you're none too good at protecting Indians. Too damn late up in Reiser Canyon, remember?"

"Yes, Johnny. I remember. You don't need to remind me of that."

"Just never forget that. Now let's get back to town." He scattered the ashes in the fire pit and then, as he was about to leave, noticed a rifle leaning against a nearby boulder.

"Sheriff, wait." He walked to the boulder, and picked up the rifle. "Sheriff, this is Swanson's also. I remember now he had two, both with the same fancy carving on the stock." He examined the rifle for a few seconds, then exclaimed, "This rifle has not been fired recently. I wonder.... " He raced to his horse and pulled Swanson's other rifle from his saddle. "This has been fired only once. Bulger took it when he left, then for some reason dropped it in the snow on his way out. Maybe one of the bullets in Swanson's body is from his own rifle. This was not a gun fight with Bulger. Colonel was murdered all right. He never fired a shot!"

"For God's sake, no chance to defend himself! Take both the guns with you, Johnny. Keep them. I'll ride to Jesse Smith tomorrow, see what he can tell me about Bulger. I'll find him as soon as possible."

Redfeather stared hard at Talbot. "You do what you can, but I got to get Mama Dillard and Amanda out of Green River. Fast! That's on me alone. Now let's go!"

They mounted their horses. Knowing there was nothing more he could say to Redfeather, Talbot motioned to Redfeather to lead, then silently followed him back down the trail toward Green River.

§

Four hours later, Johnny Redfeather stood in the middle of Courtney Dillard's room on the second floor of Milly's Saloon. He paced around the room and gestured frantically as he spoke. "Mama Courtney Dillard, doesn't make any difference why anymore. All I know is that Jake Bulger killed Colonel Swanson up in Raven Meadow, shot him and just left him to die, just like I left Bulger's brother to die at Lawton Prison. He's for sure after me, and he killed Indians up in Reiser too, so he'll kill anyone. I'm not about to leave my family behind. You, me, and Amanda got to clear out of Green River. Sheriff swears he'll find Bulger, wherever he is, but I'm not waiting on him or any other white man anymore. Now get your duffle packed in a hurry. We leave early tomorrow morning, soon as I get my guns and gear and Milly's grub ready. I told her what happened. She's wrapping a bunch of food now. I'll go tell Amanda she's coming with us."

"Why do we need her with us?"

"I told you why: she's Indian. She's not safe here anymore either. Now stop talking for once and get packed. I'm going back to Talbot's office to tell him my plans, then I'll be back here in a few hours."

"You crazy-ass red man, I knew I never should have invited you to this room on New Year's Eve! You're totally mad! Now where we going?"

"To my cabin. Raven Mountain will protect us, and we'll pray to Maheo to protect us too. Just pack and be ready when I come by tomorrow!" Redfeather slammed the door and raced down the stairs, where he met Roxy and Marilee.

"Johnny, where the hell you off to in such a hurry?" Marilee asked.

"Indian country," Redfeather yelled, and stormed out of the saloon.

23
Jesse Smith's Bunkhouse

"Sheriff, Jake Bulger isn't here," Jesse Smith said on the porch of his bunkhouse at eight o'clock the next morning. "He rode by four days ago, said he was done with herding and wanted his pay. I gave him what he was owed, and he never said where he was going. Just rode off. That's all I know. Why?"

"Well, three, maybe four days ago he killed Colonel William Swanson, a Union man, up in Raven Meadow. Seems he wanted to settle a grudge from the war involving Lawton Prison down in Georgia. Did he ever mention that?"

"Yes, I sure heard about Georgia from him, his brother, his mention of prisons. I know he was here when Tompkin had the herd, but that's about all I know about him. He didn't talk too much. Just went about his work with the cattle. He got along with the other men all right. He never mentioned being in the war, though I usually assume that everybody coming out here was involved in some way. I don't ask too many questions. Not always smart to do that."

"Yeah, I understand that. Well, if he comes back, don't tell him I was asking about him, but be damn sure to let me know. My office is in town, easy to find. Just ask around. But don't delay if he shows up. Understand?"

"Sure, Sheriff. I don't want any trouble. Been enough of that already with this herd. No need for any more."

"Much obliged," Sheriff Talbot said as he turned his horse and rode swiftly back to Green River.

§

Had Talbot returned to town a few minutes earlier he would have seen Johnny Redfeather and Courtney Dillard on one horse and Amanda on another riding slowly east toward Raven Mountain. Johnny held tightly the reins of his trusted horse, and frequently looked back at Amanda whose horse was additionally burdened by three full saddle bags of Milly's food. As they rode the rough, rocky trail toward the forest Courtney complained loudly every time she felt the baby bounce in her belly. After listening to Courtney's complaints for nearly an hour, Amanda finally shouted, "Mama, let Johnny be. He's doing what he thinks is right by us."

"Well damnit I sure hope so," Courtney said, before Redfeather shushed them both. "Stop complaining and watch the trail. Grizzlies and big cats out here, remember? Be mindful!"

As they rode Redfeather knew that he would be tempted to visit Swanson's gravesite, if only to convince himself that his and Talbot's impromptu burial had protected Swanson's corpse from whatever further degradation predators could inflict upon it. But he knew that he must resist that temptation, and get to his cabin as quickly as possible. "That's done," he thought. "Can't change it now. Too damn late." Two hours later, just as they left the forest and began riding east across the meadow, snow began falling. "God-damn snow!" he cursed loudly. "I'll be all go to hell, I sure don't want any tracks now!"

24
Union Pacific Rail Yard

Later that day Jeb Carlson bolted through the heavy wooden door of the Union Pacific bunkhouse. "Josh, where's Bulger?" he hollered. "Anyone seen him? Where is he?"

"Still out I figure," said Josh. "Ain't seen him yet for supper. Should be back soon. Don't know why he's still out there. But he usually doesn't come in with most of the other men to eat. I told him if he wants to eat, he has to be here at six-thirty, or he can go hungry."

"Well, I'll be out back having a smoke. You see him in here, tell him to come look for me. He and I got to talk."

"Sure, boss. Will do."

Ten minutes later Jake Bulger walked into the bunkhouse. "Bulger," Marquez yelled, "Jeb's looking for you. Go see him right away."

"Josh, can't I get my supper first? I'm awful hungry."

"Yeah, you're also late. I told you 'bout getting here on time. When you gonna learn?"

"Had a bunch of rocks to clear for that last track section. Couldn't get away."

"Oh yeah, then how come everybody else from that track gang has been in here and eaten? Seems you got no excuse once again. Get some grub fast and go see the boss."

Bulger grabbed a plate and filled it quickly with cold potatoes and a few strips of beef. Just as he sat down and began eating, Jeb Carlson burst through a side door.

"Bulger, put that food down and get out here! Now!"

"Jeb, what's this about?"

"I think you know!" Carlson drew his gun and pointed it at Bulger. The other men in the bunkhouse immediately scattered to its corners.

"Carlson, you got no right to pull a gun on me. I've not bothered you one bit these past few days."

"It's not me you've been bothering, Bulger. Now get outside."

Bulger put down his plate, stood, and walked slowly ahead of Carlson out the side door. When they had walked a few paces, Carlson yelled, "Stop there! Hands at your side. Turn around. And don't even think about pulling your gun!"

Hands at his side, Bulger turned to face Carlson, who still pointed a gun at his head. "All right, Bulger, now listen to me, and listen really good. I heard in Milly's today, from a waitress named Roxy, that Colonel Swanson was murdered up in Raven Meadow several days ago. Sheriff Talbot and his deputy Grogan are searching for you, and I know why. You killed Swanson, didn't you? Off on a little hunting trip to the mountains, was that it? Seems you can't let go of your revenge, can you? Got to settle scores from years ago, acting like it was yesterday. Jake, it was war, and it's over! Over for me, over for you, over for everybody. I told you that day in Hal's you can't change anything from the past, not about your brother or Redfeather or Swanson or Lawton Prison. Nothing!"

"Carlson, it wasn't your kid brother that god-damn savage left to bleed to death. Don't you lecture me!"

"Bulger, you don't know what all I lost in that war. Everybody lost something, some people a whole lot more than a kid brother. That's my business now, and that's why I'm here, middle of damn nowhere. But it's done! All of it! And more killing won't do anyone any damn good. Like you, like me, and everyone else who survived those years of slaughter, Swanson deserved a chance to live in peace without somebody trying to kill him. And that goes for Yanks as well as us Rebels!"

"You lousy Rebel turn-coat, you gone soft in the head? Forget what the god-damn Yanks did to us? Weren't just brothers, but wives, children...."

"Listen, Bulger, I lost my share. More than you or anyone else will ever know, and now I got no one left to tell it to. But I still won't have killers in this bunkhouse. We had enough of that with crazy O'Sullivan. No more!"

"You're a coward, Carlson. That's what you are!"

"Really? A coward. Then how come I'm standing here with a gun pointed at your head? Like I said, there's a lot you don't know about me, Bulger."

"Suppose you've been to Sheriff Talbot, right? Turn me in? Tell him where I am? You gonna get some reward for doin' that? Uh, that your little game now?"

Carlson cocked his pistol. "Now you listen to me, Jake Bulger. No, I did not go to Sheriff Talbot. I did not turn you in. Not yet anyway, but don't push your luck. Tomorrow's another day. This is your fight, not mine. But you aren't bunking here anymore. Pack up and go. I don't care where, but just go. I'm gonna walk you back into that bunkhouse, you're gonna grab some cold food, gather your gear, saddle up, and ride away, and I'll have this gun on you all the time you're here. Now go on. Git!"

Carlson motioned toward the door, and followed Bulger inside. The men scattered again when they entered. Carlson yelled "It's all right" as Bulger reached for his saddlebags hanging on the wall, tossed the food inside along with his bedding and his small lean-to, and walked outside. Gun still drawn, Carlson followed him to his horse. Bulger mounted, then turned his horse toward Carlson. "Jeb, don't you ever turn your back on me, 'cause if you do, I'll put a bullet right through it!"

"Yeah, I figure you would do that. That's your style, isn't it? That how you killed Swanson, in the back? Wasn't a fair fight, was it?"

"Neither was Redfeather slitting Hank's throat!" Bulger yelled and spat at Carlson's feet, then spurred his horse and rode furiously toward the mountains east of town.

25
Raven Mountain

As Redfeather, Courtney Dillard, and Amanda approached the last ridge of Raven Mountain the early evening sun was painting crimson the lingering clouds. Sunlight glanced off the glaciers below the ridge and ricocheted across the icy surface of the fearsome west wall. Light glinted off the barrel of Colonel Swanson's rifle that Johnny had strapped to the horse's left flank. Just before starting their descent to his cabin in the valley below, down the more gradually sloping east side of the mountain, Johnny stopped his horse and looked due west into the diminishing light. "Indian country," he thought. "Just us and the mountain and the sun. Nothing up here asks for reasons or explanations, and the past does not exist." He slowly urged his horse down the slippery path toward the valley below, only casually realizing that the earlier snowfall had ceased. Amanda followed closely behind on her horse.

"Mama Courtney," he began as they approached his cabin, "you and Amanda stay on these horses while I check for coyotes and other critters near the cabin. Don't want any visitors." He dismounted, and armed with Swanson's rifle walked around the perimeter of the cabin. Not finding any visitors, he returned to help Courtney off his horse and Amanda off hers. "Now help me get us set up in the cabin, just like last time. We're going to be here a while, so let's get as comfortable as we can."

"Damn you Redfeather," Courtney exclaimed as he helped her down. "You still haven't told us why exactly we're here. Why can't we stay at Milly's like other people? No damn critters as you call 'em there!"

"Mama, just hush up and get on inside, help me make us some supper. Amanda, you too."

Two hours later they sat on the small stoop at the front of the cabin.

Johnny took a swig from a whiskey bottle he had stashed in the rafters, and leaned forward.

"Now listen up, both of you. Like I've told you, I killed a young kid when Swanson and I escaped from Lawton Prison. Well, that kid's brother, Jake Bulger, is out for revenge, and he killed Colonel Swanson a few days ago while they were hunting down in the meadow. I'm convinced that he aims to kill me too, so I figured I'd better get out of Green River and take you with me. No tellin' what a man mad for revenge will do if he's desperate enough, and it might not be just me he'd try to kill. Besides, like I told you all last time, this is your Indian country too, not just mine. We're an Indian family now, and we got to protect each other. No one else will."

"Johnny, why would this man want to kill us? I didn't kill his brother, neither did Courtney," Amanda protested. "We weren't at that prison. You were!"

"Lieutenant, Jake Bulger was with Tompkin's herders when they attacked Running Bear up in Reiser Canyon. He lied to the Sheriff when he said he wasn't there. So he attacked Indians, including women and children. If he knew anything about you being Indian, no tellin' what he'd do. I just couldn't leave you and Mama in town while I was up here. How I see it is we got to be together. That's the safest way."

"So we're up here and some mad man from the war still wants to kill every damn Indian he can find. That's what you're telling me now," exclaimed Courtney. "Just cause this kid is yours, as near as I can figure, this Bulger maniac would kill me too?"

"I don't know that for sure, but I figure you're safer here than in town. Like I said, revenge can twist a man's mind, make him want to kill everything he can touch. Colonel Swanson is dead because Jake Bulger won't forgive him something that happened in the war three years ago. And since it was me that killed that kid, he sure as hell won't forgive me. Never! It's not rattlesnakes I'm worried about. It's walking snakes like Bulger."

"Well, just how damn long we gonna be here?" Courtney demanded.

"Don't know for sure. Sheriff Talbot and his deputy are trying to find Bulger, but there's no way to know how long that will take. We just got to stay here and be careful. Amanda, I'm entrusting you with Colonel Swanson's rifle. You go anywhere from this cabin, even to forage for berries or whatever, you take that rifle with you, and use it if you have to.

Just like back at Milly's I'm trusting you to help protect us and this little place."

"And like I said back then, I'm proud to serve," Amanda affirmed.

"Good. Just one more thing. When I took Colonel Swanson hunting I brought him to this cabin. Only white man ever been up here, as best I know. Jake Bulger killed Swanson in that meadow below, but I trust Swanson wouldn't have told him about my place. So there's no reason for him to believe I'm here. Only thing I'm worried about is those damn tracks my horse made in the snow today. I sure as hell hadn't figured on snow. But it's done, so if Bulger comes back to this meadow, he might see our tracks. So we got to be right careful. Understand?"

"I reckon," Amanda replied.

"Now it's getting' late, and cold. Let's get the bedrolls and blankets out. Time to sleep."

They stepped inside, and as Courtney and Amanda began arranging their bedding, Johnny pulled his four arrows from their leather satchel hanging near the front door. He walked outside to the large stone circle he had laid out months before and placed one arrow at each of the four directions just as he had done previously. He then moved to the center of the smaller stone ring, knelt, and prayed. "Maheo, this night, taa'eva, protect my family." He knelt for a long time, until the crisp night air had penetrated his bones. He then gathered his arrows, went inside, and lay under the wool blanket on his cot next to Courtney. He reached over to her and gently stroked her fertile belly under the blanket. "Neneso, your child," he murmured. "Naneso, my child. Maheo'o, our house." Courtney reached out and held his hand.

26

Johnny Redfeather's Cabin

Johnny awoke at sunrise. He slipped from under the blanket he shared with Courtney who, like Amanda, remained sleeping. He removed his arrows from their leather satchel and took from a post near the door a silver chain with its turquoise bear paw medallion and hung it around his neck. He put on his buffalo-skin moccasins, and walked out the front door of his cabin. He approached the stone circle and began walking slowly around it. At each of the four directions he again pointed an arrow to the sun before placing it on the ground: red painted arrows north-south, black painted arrows east-west. The brilliant light caressing the eastern slopes of Raven Mountain created a shadowy companion as he walked, as if, he thought, Maheo the Creator would hear the prayers of not one, but two Cheyenne braves performing their ritual ceremony as best they could.

One hour later, Courtney appeared at the door of the cabin. "Johnny," she called, "stop walking around in circles and get on in here! Me and Amanda are hungry as hell, and my baby is kicking too. Where'd you put the bacon and eggs that Milly gave you? We got to eat!"

"Yes, sweet Mama Dillard. Right away!" Johnny exclaimed as he walked up to her and kissed her. "Papa Redfeather is about to take care of his family. Tell Amanda to collect some kindling, and I'll get the stove going. We'll eat real soon."

"Then what? What we gonna do up here all day? Talk about more monsters again?"

"We'll go down into the next valley over below the cabin. I'll show you where to gather some herbs and flowers to make some nice teas. There's a trail that starts just behind the cabin. Bears like that valley too, so I'll take my rifle in case we run into mama grizzly again or some big cat. Maybe get us a deer. Lots to do. Not too cold, so we're probably not getting any more snow. Should be a real fine day up here."

"Yeah, well it better be! This still isn't my idea of a pleasant place, and I'm scared stiff of those snakes and critters you're always goin' on about. Amanda doesn't like them either."

"Now Mama, no snakes will bother us here. I told you, we're up too high. And if any do happen to slither over the mountain, I'll shoot every damn one of them. Now let's get inside so I can start that fire."

§

Although Jake Bulger had hoped to spend several more days at the railroad bunkhouse while he schemed how to kill Redfeather, he realized now that he had little time to find him. He also knew that he was now willing to risk his own life to kill him. Since Sheriff Talbot knew that Swanson had gone hunting with him, and by now certainly would have begun looking for him, Bulger knew that he could not risk going back to Green River where he had initially hoped to find and kill Redfeather. After leaving the railroad camp he had ridden into the early evening, and despite his near encounter with what he was sure had been a grizzly bear after killing Swanson, he had bedded down at the edge of the forest rather than ride further in darkness. The next morning, after a quick breakfast of stale biscuits, he checked his supply of ammunition and then began riding slowly in a zig-zag, generally eastern direction into the snow-covered meadow. He remembered hearing Talbot say at Milly's that Redfeather probably had a cabin somewhere up in these mountains, and he knew that he would not be in Reiser Canyon. He also knew that he was gambling that because Redfeather had taken Swanson hunting in Raven Meadow, therefore his cabin might well be either somewhere nearby or possibly farther up the mountain.

After nearly two hours riding in the meadow Bulger spotted what looked like depressions in the snow ahead of him. Increasing his pace, he found the tracks of two horses walking slowly east toward the foothills. He remembered that he and Swanson had ridden north out of the forest, and guessed that these recent tracks were almost certainly those of Redfeather heading east to his cabin. "Who else would be up here?" he wondered out loud. "And ain't this something'? New snow giving me just what I need. Tracks! So, red man, now I think I know how to find you. And when I do, I will make sure you suffer a nice, slow, painful death, just like that bastard Swanson. And if you got company up on that mountain, as it seems you might, don't matter as long as I get you. Might take a few more bullets is all, just like at Reiser. Don't matter how many, or what it costs me anymore." As he rode images of his brother lying bleeding on the dusty floor of Lawton Prison flashed through his mind. "Hank, Hank, I'll get that savage, I swear I will," he shouted.

Bulger rode more quickly now, following the two sets of tracks. As he ascended the foothills the snow deepened, and the further he rode the more he suspected that if Redfeather's cabin were at the end of this path it was increasingly likely to be somewhere near the top of Raven Mountain. "Way the hell up a mountain, what for?" he wondered. "How's a man supposed to live up here? Grizzlies and mountain lions for company. Just another savage I guess. Maybe the only place he can live."

The horses' tracks wound south-east up the foothills. As Bulger approached the steep southern flank of the mountain the trail he was determined to follow became increasingly treacherous. His horse stumbled frequently on the slippery rocks beneath the snow. As he gazed at the two huge protruding arms of glacial ice and rock he sensed that he was entering an alien environment. Massive chunks of ice, loosened by the warming sun, cracking and cascading down the west wall carrying boulders to snow fields below, unnerved him. "Crazy dangerous place," he muttered. Not seeing any decent camp sites on the increasingly steep route up to the summit, Bulger resigned himself to spending one more night alone, this time high on the mountain. For three more hours he plodded up the rugged southern flank, stopping frequently to assure himself that he was actually seeing a path upward through the melting snow and rocks littering the landscape. As he approached the ridge line south of the summit, the heavier snow yielded more readily the tracks of the horses he was following. He could see tracks continuing up and then across the summit before sloping more gradually downward and then disappearing below the ridge. "So somewhere down there, Johnny Redfeather. That's where your little cabin must be," he thought as he looked down the slope as far as he could. "Early tomorrow morning I will ride down there and if I find you, savage man, I'll kill you. Finally!"

Just below the summit, out of the biting wind, Bulger decided to camp for the night. Rather than risk signaling his presence with a fire, he elected to eat only the few remaining biscuits he had grabbed at the railroad bunkhouse. "Hank, Hank," he murmured as he waved his hands around to try to warm himself, "no way I'm stopping now. No way. This cold is nothing!" He made sure his Remington was fully loaded, then crawled under a heavy wool blanket next to a large boulder that he hoped would shield him from the wind.

Near the eastern edge of the forest far below, Hestovatohkeo'o emerged from a grove of white pines. With one face he gazed back down Bulger's tracks through the forest, and with the other at the summit of Raven Mountain.

27
FINAL MEETING

The next morning, after completing yet another ceremonial dance around the larger stone circle, Johnny Redfeather walked back into the cabin and hung his arrows and silver chain on the hook near the front door. Courtney and Amanda were already cooking eggs and bacon on a small grill in the fireplace. He brushed snow off his moccasins. "Damn, but that smells good!" he exclaimed as he walked toward the fire to warm his hands. "Glad to see you two have mastered cooking in that old fireplace. Maybe later this summer I'll gather some more rocks and build a bigger one."

"You do that, Johnny Redfeather," Courtney replied. "Even with this little grill this one's almost too small to cook over. Can hardly cook even one slab of bacon at a time! You don't expect me to cook over this thing all the while we're up here, do you? And by the way, you still haven't told me and Amanda how long you're planning on staying here. It was cold last night, and this is no place for a baby, even if its father is an Indian."

"Now Mama, don't get all excited again. We're just going to be here for a little while. We got to give Sheriff Talbot time to find Bulger. I don't know how long exactly that will take, but I believe that we're safer here for several days than we would be in town. Now quit worrying and let's eat some of that bacon and eggs you got frying there. No use letting it get cold while we waste time talking about what we can't do anything about. Isn't that right, Lieutenant?"

"I reckon, if you say so, Johnny. Yeah, let's eat! Oh, and afterwards Courtney and I want to go back down the trail behind the cabin to that lower valley where we walked last time we stayed here. That's real pretty. Maybe get some more herbs, maybe pick some of them wildflowers you told us about too. Maybe make the cabin smell really nice. That all right with you?"

"Yeah, that's fine, I guess. I'll stay here and cut some firewood out in front of the cabin. That way I would see anyone coming down the trail from the summit above. Take Colonel Swanson's rifle with you, but don't go firing it just for the hell of it. Just be careful is all. The sun today is already hotter than it was yesterday and most of that snow will melt fast, so you won't have trouble walking down or back up the trail. And if mama grizzly and her little ones are down in that valley, just stay away and leave her alone. She won't bother you if you don't bother her. But don't stay too long. I'll be out front guarding the cabin."

"I reckon," Amanda agreed.

§

Redfeather carried his hatchet and gun belt out to a scattering of pine logs a short distance from the front of his cabin. He slung the gun belt over a tree limb and, with his back to the trail above him, began chopping off branches and stashing them in small piles near the front of the cabin. One hour later he heard scraping noises and the rumble of stones behind him. He whirled around. A few yards away, Jake Bulger stood above him pointing a rifle at his chest.

"So, Johnny Redfeather, this is your little hideout! How nice of you to leave me those tracks to follow! Didn't expect such a courtesy from a cold-blooded savage! And don't bother reaching for those pistols you left hanging on that branch over there. Won't do you no good now."

Redfeather stood still, his right hand frozen on the hatchet. "Bulger! How the hell did you find me here?"

"Well, wasn't all that hard. But I had a little help from your friend Colonel Swanson on our hunting trip. He told me you had taken him hunting in that meadow down there. I figured your cabin had to be near here. Course I knew it was a gamble. But I figured it was worth a try."

"Swanson! Swanson! You're lying, Bulger. He'd never betray me. He...."

"Ha! Well I'll just let you fret about that while I put some bullets into your rotten body so you bleed to death nice and slow. Just like you done to my brother Hank at Lawton Prison."

"Lawton! Bulger, that was war! He jumped me from behind and

tried to kill me. I just defended myself. That's exactly what happened!"

"You left him to die!"

"You know god-damn well you would have done the same to escape. Any soldier would have!"

"Maybe, maybe not. Don't matter now. All that matters is that I'm going to shoot you and then stand here and watch you bleed to death. Just like I did Swanson. Seems you got no company here just now so I can wait a few minutes till your blood is all over the stones and snow. Be real pretty I believe! Then I'm going to head back up this damn mountain trail and forget I ever spent time finding and killing you. Then Hank's ghost will leave me in peace."

"You kill men in cold blood you'll become the savage you god-damn white men keep calling us Indians."

"You lousy half-breed! What the hell you know about white men? You're red all the way down. Now where do you want the first one?"

"Bulger, listen to me. I'm raisin' a girl, just thirteen, and my lady is pregnant. You kill me, and those children will be without a father. Is that your idea of revenge? Is that going to make you a man? You think that's what your brother's ghost wants you to do? Deprive kids of their father?"

"So now you want me to give a damn about little Indian kids, huh? Is that right? "

"Bulger, too many Indian children have died! Up at Reiser Canyon most all the children in Running Bear's tribe were shot to death. They had no chance! Just butchered! You ever see anything like that? A whole valley full of dying children bleeding and screaming? You got any idea what that's like? Any idea at all?"

"Yeah, Redfeather, I got a real good idea. I was there. Shot as many of them little red shits as I could."

"You god-damn barbarian! You lousy white bas…." Bulger fired bullets into both of Redfeather's thighs. As he fell backward, Bulger fired into both his arms. "Bleed red, savage! Bleed red! I'll just stand here and watch."

Writhing in pain, frantically thrashing his limbs in pools of blood, Redfeather screamed, "Amanda! Mama Courtney! Neneso! Naneso! Maheo'o! Arrows, red, black! Swanson, betray! No! Maheo, Hestovatohkeo'o, come, come…."

"Jesus, Redfeather," Bulger laughed, "you crazy savage, you can't even die right! Shit, I ain't gonna waste any more time listening to your gibberish. Time to go. So long, you lousy Indian bastard. Have a nice, slow death." Staring at Redfeather's writhing body, Bulger paused. "All right, Hank. I'm done. Got 'em both!" After firing several shots at the cabin, he strode quickly up the trail to his horse tethered to a large tree stump fifty yards away. He mounted and violently whipped the animal as it raced wildly toward the crest of Raven Mountain.

Having heard the gun shots half a mile down the trail, Amanda and Courtney raced up the valley to the cabin. Amanda ran around the corner and saw Johnny first. "Mama Dillard, here! Out front!" Courtney stumbled to the front of the cabin and, seeing the bloodied body, screamed, "Johnny! Johnny! No! Johnny! Johnny! No! No!" She ran to Redfeather and hurled herself onto his blood-soaked torso. Hysterically repeating his name, she pressed her hands above his leg wounds, trying frantically to stop the bleeding. "Stop! Stop! Stop!" she screamed at his wounds, vainly ordering them to cease flowing. After several minutes of raging uncontrollably at the futility of her efforts, she began sobbing and methodically mopping up blood with the melting snow and her skirt. "Too late, Mama. Too late," Redfeather mumbled, and gasping in pain lifted his right hand to her womb. "Neneso, naneso, your child, my child. Mama, raise it right. Indian. Remember. Maheo," he cried as he desperately clutched her womb, "protect our child! Mama...."

"Johnny, you can't die! I Love you! Husband! Johnny! Johnny Redfeather!" She took his head in her bloodied hands, and caressed his cheeks. "Johnny Redfeather, you crazy Indian! Why did you bring us here? Why? You said...."

Amanda, choking back tears and barely able to speak, knelt at Redfeather's feet. "Mama Courtney, too late. He's dead.," she sputtered. "He's dead, Mama Courtney! It isn't possible, but it is! Johnny Redfeather is dead! Dead!" Amanda pounded the earth with her fists, then with both hands furiously scrawled the bloody dirt across her face until her cheeks and forehead bled. She bent over, lay her face on the earth, and pulled madly on her hair, trying to rip it from her head. "Indian hair," she screamed. "Johnny said I had Indian hair. How can I have Indian hair if Johnny Redfeather is dead? That's not possible now!" She lay prone on the ground, sobbing, convulsing. Courtney, moaning, shaking, continued to stroke Redfeather's cheeks.

After several minutes, Amanda looked up. "The tracks, Mama. The tracks in the snow! Not Johnny's fault. Bulger followed the tracks in the damn snow. Let Johnny go in peace now. We need to get him down the mountain, to Eagle Canyon. His soul has to go to Seana, like Johnny once told me the souls of Cheyenne warriors go. Come on. Let's wash him, then we got to somehow get him up on his horse. As Johnny would say, 'I'll be all go to hell, but it's a long way down.' And we got to be really careful. It must be this guy Bulger that killed Johnny. He's heading down the mountain, and no tellin' where we'll meet him. But we have to take that chance. Have to keep an eye, have Johnny's guns ready. Come on, Mama. We have to do this. You and I will ride Johnny's horse, and we'll have to get his body up onto the other horse. I'll get the horses ready. And we have to take his arrows. I'll go get them. Come on now, Mama Courtney. No good staying here now."

For several more minutes Courtney Dillard lay beside Johnny Redfeather's corpse, crying and vainly stroking his cheeks, kissing his lips and his forehead, as if her lips could give him life. "Johnny, Johnny, Johnny...." Sobbing uncontrollably, she began wiping his wounds with her skirt just as Amanda returned with Redfeather's arrows and two blankets and knelt beside her.

Suddenly a fierce, frenzied wind whipping dust and snow swirled from off the crest of Raven Mountain. Massive black clouds appeared and obliterated the sun. Streaks of lightning shot across the darkened sky, colliding and igniting the very air, and monstrous thunder clasps caromed among the peaks and valleys below. Terrified, Courtney and Amanda huddled together at Redfeather's feet and covered their heads. "The mountain knows. It's angry!" Amanda screamed into the relentless whirlwind. "It's angry at the killing of Johnny Redfeather!" She covered Courtney with one of Redfeather's blankets and pulled her underneath, then lay across her as the thunder roared and the lightning crackled.

"Mama, Mama," Amanda whispered several minutes later as the early morning calm gradually returned.

§

Jake Bulger had just reached the crest of Raven Mountain when the freakish storm exploded above him. Suddenly unable to see the way forward, he halted his horse and clung to its neck to calm the animal as it whinnied furiously and tottered on the narrow, rocky trail. For several minutes horse and rider, no longer distinct figures, cowered beneath the elements surging above and around them and disappeared amid the whirling snow and dust. "Crazy god-damn mountain," Bulger yelled. "Leave me alone! leave me alone! I just want to get out of here!" When the storm subsided, Bulger slowly resumed guiding his horse forward across the mountain. Approaching the southern flank he rode cautiously over the uneven ground, aware that in places lingering snow might hide treacherous rocks. Confidant in his ability to escape any punishment for having killed Redfeather, Bulger now saw no reason to hurry his ride.

As he descended, the snow that had provided the tracks to Redfeather's cabin was melting fast under the brilliant sun, and the longer he rode the more concerned he became about finding his path down among the boulders strewn haphazardly across the landscape. While he knew he was going down the same mountain he had climbed the day before, nonetheless he became increasingly uneasy about the exact route he had taken. Even at somewhat lower elevations, where there was less snow cover, landmarks he thought he had noticed when climbing, like peculiar rock formations or a sudden narrowing of the trail, now seemed to have disappeared. Left seemed right; right seemed left. As he gazed back up the mountain its massive arms, menacing agents of a power unique onto itself, seemed poised to pull him into its frigid core.

One hour after Bulger started down the southern flank, high winds again began scouring snow off the summit. Within minutes, a howling blizzard enveloped the entire mountain in whirling whiteness. Startled by another sudden storm, Bulger looked up and to his right, and through the blinding snow he dimly perceived a monstrous black figure striding steadily toward him from above. Bulger froze in abject terror, his mouth suddenly dry, his heart racing. "Who are you? What are you? You ain't no god-damn grizzly! What do you want? What are you?" he screamed at the creature. Just as he reached for his rifle his panicked horse reared, then bolted. It immediately stumbled amid a pile of rocks and fell, sending Bulger sprawling toward a cliff. He looked up. Towering above him, the huge creature turned its head to reveal a second, hideous face. Hearing a deafening roar, Bulger saw a wall of rock and ice thundering toward him. "No, no!" he screamed, and a massive avalanche careening down the southern flank of Raven Mountain swept man and horse into oblivion.

§

Two hours later Amanda, gingerly leading Redfeather's horse down the mountain, suddenly halted. "Mama Dillard," she said, turning to Courtney, "look here." She pointed to a steep section of the trail washed clean of rocks and snow where debris had obviously plunged over the edge. "An avalanche has been through here since we came up. Good thing we're slow, or it might have gotten us. I wonder if that got Bulger. His horse's tracks end here, though the avalanche might have come down after he passed. But if we don't see his tracks further down, I'll be all go to hell but Johnny's mountain took care of Bulger for good. Maybe took him and his horse over the cliff right down there. Could be now we won't have to worry about him anymore. You think so, Courtney?"

"Yeah, Amanda, serves him right I guess, if that's what happened. Don't know that I can quite think about that now. I'm just thinking about Johnny Redfeather's dead body lying on that horse behind us. Not room in my mind for anything else right now."

"Sure, Mama Courtney. I understand. All we got to do now is get him down this mountain and in to town, then out to Eagle Canyon. And we can't linger here. Come on, horse. Take Johnny Redfeather home."

§

Later that afternoon Milly and Frank helped Courtney and Amanda lift Redfeather's body off his horse, then carried it into a small room at the back of the saloon. Marilee tried vainly to comfort Courtney, who, despite her grieving, insisted on helping the women prepare Redfeather's body for burial. Frank went to Doctor Johnson's office up the street and, when he heard what had happened, he agreed to come to Milly's immediately and dress the wounds as best he could. Once Johnson had finished, Milly, Marilee and Courtney washed the body again, then wrapped it in clean sheets and a heavy blanket for the ride to Eagle Canyon. Johnson agreed to have his buggy ready by ten o'clock the next morning, and Milly agreed to close the Green River Saloon all the next day. "Can't be open when we're burying Johnny Redfeather," she proclaimed.

After they finished cleaning and wrapping the body, and after Courtney had eaten a small supper, Marilee helped her up the stairs to her room. That night Amanda slept with Courtney, wiping her tears with a clean cloth and promising that she would help her raise Johnny's Indian child.

28
Eagle Canyon

"Sheriff, I didn't know you knew all that," Jeb Carlson said as he sat in Talbot's office the next morning.

"Yeah, Johnny figured it all out when we found Swanson's body. He had scrawled 'lawton' and 'bulger' in the snow before he died, and Johnny knew right away what it meant. Johnny killed Bulger's kid brother in Lawton just before he and Swanson escaped. Kid jumped on his back and Johnny slit his throat."

"Yeah, that's what Bulger told me in late April up at Hal's. Guess I should have told you something about him then. I told him I wanted nothing to do with whatever he was planning. I also reminded him that the war was over, and that there was no need for revenge now. Too damn late. But I obviously couldn't persuade him to let it alone. I just didn't want to get involved in his business. But I sure wish I had told you sooner what he told me. I guess I didn't really believe he would kill them both. I sure am sorry, Sheriff. I kicked him out of the bunkhouse soon as I heard from Roxy at Milly's that Swanson was dead. I knew Bulger had killed him."

"Well, if Swanson had known who Bulger was he sure as hell wouldn't have gone hunting with him. But too damn late now. Seems lately that's the way with trying to do what's right out here. Always too late."

"Speaking of Bulger, you got any idea where he is? He didn't come back to the bunkhouse."

"Well, no, but I've got a pretty good idea. Amanda said she saw where an avalanche had come down the mountain's south flank when they were bringing Johnny's body down. She said the tracks of Bulger's horse stopped after they passed that area. Seems he's at the bottom of a gigantic pile of ice and rocks somewhere deep in Raven Mountain. I've already been to Smith's place earlier this morning just to be sure, but he said Bulger did not return yesterday."

Doctor Mark Johnson knocked on the door frame. Talbot motioned for him to enter. "Well, Jeb, if you'll excuse me, we got a funeral to take care of this morning. Doc, this is Jeb Carlson. Jeb, Doctor Mark Johnson." The men shook hands. "Well, Sheriff, I'll be going. Guess there's nothing more I can do here. Wish I'd done more sooner."

"Don't we all, Jeb? Don't we all? Thanks for coming in."

"Doctor Johnson, pleased to meet you," Carlson added as he left Talbot's office.

"Jim, what did Carlson mean 'do more'"?

"Well, Doc, he told me he knew back in April that Bulger was after Swanson and Redfeather for killing his kid brother at Lawton. He just wishes now he had told me about Bulger months ago. Might have stopped Bulger before he killed them both. Can't know for sure, of course, and I can't arrest a man for holding a deadly grudge. But still...."

"Oh for Christ's sake, Jim. Why the hell didn't he...?"

"Said he didn't want to get involved in Bulger's business. Like everyone else I guess, he's just trying to put everything from the war behind him, including personal desires for revenge. Can't say I blame him for that."

"Well, guess not. What's done is done. I got my buggy and two horses outside. Guess we should be going."

"Yeah, best get this over with. Let's drive over to Milly's. I'll ride along with you."

Marilee greeted Talbot and Johnson as they reached the saloon, and approached Jim immediately. "Jim, I'd like to ride along, for Courtney's sake. She's going to need someone with her. Milly's will be closed all day, so no need to stay here."

"Sure, Marilee. I understand. Is the body ready?"

"Yes, it's all done. We washed it last night after Doc finished, then wrapped it in some clean sheets and a blanket Milly had. It's not fancy, but it's about the best we could do in a hurry. Amanda didn't want the undertaker anywhere near Johnny. She said this has to be done Indian way, not white man's."

"That seems right. Let's get Johnny loaded onto Doc's carriage." Frank and Sam emerged from the saloon carrying the body. Milly,

Courtney and Amanda walked beside it. Amanda, sobbing, carried a leather satchel over her left shoulder. Courtney, crying softly, repeatedly stroked Redfeather's corpse as she whispered "Johnny, Johnny." Frank and Sam placed the body in the back of Johnson's carriage, and Courtney and Amanda got in and sat on either side of it.

"You about ready?" Johnson asked. "Yes," Courtney mumbled, "We're ready."

"We'll be here when you get back," Milly said. "You all do right now by Johnny Redfeather," she urged and buried her tearful face in her hands. Frank put his arm around her, trying to calm her shaking body. Sam stood by the back of the carriage, sobbing softly. "Nothin' ever gonna be the same now. Not without Johnny Redfeather," he said to the indifferent air.

Marilee climbed onto the front seat of Johnson's carriage and sat between him and Talbot. Johnson flicked the reins, and the carriage moved slowly up the dusty street.

§

They arrived at the north rim of Eagle Canyon at noon. On the west wall the stream above Casper Bluff, still flush with snow melt, careened down its rocky path toward the immense canyon below. The sun caressed the canyon's walls while straining to penetrate its mysterious depths. Amanda jumped off the carriage and walked to the canton rim. "We got to take him to the bottom of the canyon," she said. "He told me this canyon is sacred to Indians, so we have to take him down there to rest. Can't leave him up here."

"Won't be easy, but if you say so we can do that," Talbot responded. "We'll all help."

"It's a long way," Amanda added. "But we have to do this."

Talbot and Johnson slowly slid Redfeather's body out of the back of the carriage and held it aloft. "Amanda, Courtney, grab hold of the sheets," Talbot urged. "We'll walk slowly. It looks steep, and the rocks are probably still wet from dew and snow melt. Take our time. Marilee, please walk in front, guide us down."

They walked slowly, deliberately into the depths of Eagle Canyon, Marilee occasionally alerting them to loose rocks or errant streams they would have to cross. Three hours later, after several rest stops, they reached the bottom and stopped near a small, still pond created by rocks and downed logs in the stream. "Here," Courtney said, and they lowered Redfeather's body. "Marilee, Amanda, unwrap the blanket then help wash the sheets. They got dusty on the trail. Just take a few minutes."

Talbot and Johnson stepped aside as the three women carried water in their cupped hands from the stream and washed as much of the dust as they could from the shroud. Amanda then removed Redfeather's four arrows from their leather satchel. She placed one of the red-painted arrows at the head and foot of the corpse, and one of the black-painted on either side. She then walked slowly around the corpse, stopping at each of the arrows and touching it, then raising it upward before replacing it. When she finished walking, she pleaded, "Maheo, Maheo, bless Johnny Redfeather on his journey home." Amanda and Marilee then stood next to Courtney as she carefully unwound the cloth from around Redfeather's head and, gently stroking his cheeks, kissed his lips and forehead. "Cold, Johnny. Cold," she whispered, sobbing. "You're cold. Never once knew you to be cold, my Johnny dear. Never." As she had at his cabin, Amanda bent over and took Courtney's heaving shoulders in her hands. "Courtney, Courtney. We have to leave Johnny Redfeather alone now. He's at rest. Come on, now. Like he told me here, his spirit has to go on its journey to Seana. We can't get in the way. Come on now Mama. You and your baby...."

"Naneso!" Courtney suddenly raged. "Johnny Redfeather, neneso, neneso, your child! Johnny!" She screamed, and clasped her hands tightly over her womb. After several seconds Amanda slowly lifted Courtney, and she and Marilee led her back from the pond to where the men were standing.

"Courtney, hush now," Marilee said. "We'll bury Johnny right. You'll see. It's all we can do now."

"Marilee's right," Amanda whispered to Courtney, holding her tightly. "Best we get on with it."

"Jim," Marilee pleaded. "You and Doc help us bury Johnny. We'll wash his face, then wrap his body tight again. Gather some stones and some dirt, and cover him as best we can. Amanda told me last night what we have to do. Then we have to start back up. It's a long, steep climb and the sun is really hot."

Marilee held Courtney as Jim, Doc Johnson, and Amanda gathered stones and placed them around the perimeter of the body. They packed dirt and smaller pebbles between the stones. Amanda then closed the cloth over Redfeather's face for the last time.

"Johnny," Courtney mumbled, and reached for his body. "No," Marilee said, holding her back. "Courtney, no more. Leave Johnny Redfeather in peace. We have to do this. Please. Come on now. We have to go."

"I'll be all go to hell, but now Johnny will go on his journey to Seana. Just like he told me," Amanda said, "We did right by him. Goodbye, Johnny Redfeather."

"Jim," Marilee pleaded, "help Courtney now. We have to get back to the carriage and get her back to Milly's. It's hot and the trail is steep. We have to start up right away. Please help her."

"Of course, Marilee. Whatever you say." Talbot held Courtney for several minutes as she sobbed into his chest. Then, holding her by the arm, he led her slowly away from the gravesite as they started walking up the trail.

Nearly five hours later, as the sun slipped behind gathering clouds, they reached the rim of the canyon. Johnson and Talbot helped Courtney onto the front seat of the carriage, where she would sit between them for the ride back to town. Amanda and Marilee sat in the back holding each other's hands as they wept. Johnson flicked the reins, and they began riding toward Green River.

From high above the solemn company shrieks of a bird of prey echoed through Eagle Canyon.

29
Departure

Twelve months later, at 10:00 AM on Sunday, June 21st, a rickety old buggy drawn by a single shaggy horse ambled away from the front of Milly's Saloon toward the south end of town. Several people stood on the steps of the saloon and waved at the departing travelers. Seated in the back among several duffle bags and a large basket of food was a woman cradling a nine month old infant wrapped in a cotton blanket. The woman wore a red and white calico dress, a white shawl over her shoulders, and a large straw hat to shield her baby from the blazing summer sun. Behind the wagon a large horse, bearing a young girl, trotted slowly.

After a few minutes the driver looked back at the woman who was seated on a small bench.

"You all right back there, Courtney?"

"Yes, Butch. I'm fine. Johnny Redarrow is all right too. He's just fine. We'll have to stop in a few miles. I'll have to feed him. Maybe we can find a shady spot with some water, like a small stream."

"Sure thing, Courtney. Whatever you say."

Epilogue

A nation is not conquered
Until the hearts of its women are on the ground.
Then it is finished,
No matter how brave its warriors
Or how strong their weapons.
Cheyenne proverb

Readers Guide

1. Raven Mountain: A Mythic Novel, is the sequel to Green River Saga, which Sunstone Press published in April, 2020. In fact, chapter one of Raven Mountain begins immediately after the end of Green River Saga. While the Preface to Raven Mountain provides some background on Johnny Redfeather, its central character, readers should, at the very least, read carefully the last chapter of Green River Saga to understand Redfeather's state of mind at the beginning of this sequel.

2. The acknowledgments page in Raven Mountain includes Peter Cozzens's book The Earth is Weeping, which chronicles the long and tortuous history of the "Indian Wars" in the Western United States, both before and especially after the Civil War. To better appreciate Redfeather at the beginning of this novel, read especially Cozzens's account of the Sand Creek Massacre, the fate of Cheyenne chief Black Kettle, and the subsequent dispersal of many Native American tribes following Sand Creek.

3. Johnny Redfeather is of mixed European-Native American heritage: his father was Irish; his mother was Cheyenne and the daughter of a Medicine Man, an important role in Native American societies. As you read Raven Mountain ask yourself how difficult you believe it would have been for Redfeather to maintain his Cheyenne heritage amid the rapid expansion of white settlements and the increasing conflicts that Cozzens narrates. Then, engage in dialogues with local Native people about how they try to maintain their native culture amid dominating

white society today; and also talk with immigrants who try to sustain their cultural heritage while trying to "fit into" what is for them a foreign society. Has reading Raven Mountain at all affected your own thinking about these issues? If so, how?

4. Raven Mountain covers several months in 1867, two years after the end of the Civil War. Given question # 3, and despite the book's historical setting, in what ways might this novel be considered relevant to contemporary American society?

5. The Greek word Mythos means "story." However, Mythos does not intrinsically indicate whether a story is true or false. While all literature is fictional—i.e., its stories did not literally, or actually happen—literature is nonetheless psychologically true because its many forms tell us about our enormously complex human nature. Discuss the many places where Johnny Redfeather tells Courtney Dillard, Amanda, and Colonel Swanson about Cheyenne myths and then consider: 1) how these myths constitute a parallel narrative throughout the novel; 2) why these myths are crucial to Redfeather's efforts to maintain his Cheyenne identity and heritage; and 3) for the legend of Hestovatokheo'o, in English "Two Face," in what sense are some of the legends that Redfeather relates, especially one in particular, true?

6. Why, and where, does Johnny Redfeather dance alone? Or, is he alone? What Cheyenne ceremony is he trying to recreate, to whom does he pray while dancing, and why are his dance and praying so important for him?

7. Although there are several extant versions of the Cheyenne story of the Sacred Arrows, they generally agree about the role of the Creator—in Cheyenne language Maheo, or Ma'heo'o, "The Holy One." Why for Johnny is the deific origin of these stories so important? What similarities exist between the Sacred Arrow stories and the sacred texts, or stories, of the three major Abrahamic religions?

8. Lame Deer, the Sioux Medicine Man quoted in the epigraph, insists that "The Earth is a living thing. The Mountains speak." Identify the environmental ethos present in Lame Deer's words, and explain fully how and exactly where Raven Mountain is itself a character in the novel.

How is the mountain present in the two parallel narratives of the novel: the sequence of events, and Redfeather's Cheyenne myths?

9. "Snuffy" appears in Green River Saga as an orphan living in Milly's Saloon. Why in Raven Mountain does Redfeather take her to Eagle Canyon? Who were her parents? How is she similar to Redfeather? And to Johnny's and Courtney's child? What is significant about his telling her there that from that point on she is to be known as Amanda? She is 13 years old; where in the novel does she show exceptional maturity for a girl her age?

10. Evaluate the author's use of Cheyenne language in his portrait of Johnny Redfeather. Is this "second language" important to Redfeather's character? Are there places in the novel where the Cheyenne language is especially effective portraying Redfeather? How is your answer here related to how you answered question # 3? How important is language to minority cultures; i.e., Spanish in English-dominated Anglo America?

11. Trace the evolving relationship between Johnny Redfeather and Courtney Dillard, whom he often calls, to her annoyance, "Darla." What does she call him in the penultimate scene at his cabin, and what does that word tell us about her at the end of the book? Conversely, how do other men in the novel describe her?

12. Discuss thoroughly Jake Bulger's character and his motives for revenge. Is he in any sense "justified" for his actions? How did his brother Hank die? He tells Jeb Carlson in Hal's Saloon in chapter three that he seeks revenge against Redfeather for his brother's death, but is that all that motivates him? Consider Edward Westermarck's assertion quoted in the epigraph that revenge is "essentially rooted in the feeling of power and superiority." Does war "excuse" violent acts that occur away from actual battle?

13. The narrative "arc" of Raven Mountain is essentially tragic. Several characters make mistakes—some major, some minor—that lead to the tragedy. As an exercise in analyzing the novel's structure, explain how the mistakes of Johnny Redfeather, Colonel William Swanson, Sheriff JimTalbot, and Jeb Carlson, a minor figure, contribute to the conclusion.

14. The tracks in the snow leading up Raven Mountain are crucial in the final portion of the book. Explain thoroughly the role of this unexpected snow fall and its complex irony in the fate of Johnny Redfeather and his "family" of Courtney Dillard and Amanda. How is your discussion of this irony relevant to study question # 7?

15. The author has lived amid the rugged mountains of the Pacific Northwest for 41 years. Are his descriptions of the mountain environment sufficiently evocative that you sense the actual presence of the mountains in the novel? What particular passages seem successful in this endeavor?

Printed in the USA
CPSIA information can be obtained
at www.ICGtesting.com
LVHW032058281123
765126LV00004B/157

9 781632 935571